I0633129

# THE DANGER WITH LOVE

AMANDA SIEGRIST

Copyright © 2017 Amanda Siegrist
All Rights Reserved.

This material may not be re-produced, re-formatted, or copied in any
format for sale or personal use unless given permission by the publisher.

NO AI TRAINING: No part of this material may be used in any AI training
of any kind. Without in any way limiting the Author's exclusive rights
under copyright, any use of this publication to "train" generative artificial
intelligence (AI) technologies to generate text is expressly prohibited. The
Author reserves all rights to license any and all use of this work for
generative AI training and development of machine learning language
models.

Every part of this material was human created, including all written words
and the cover.

All characters in this book are a product of the author's imagination. Places,
events, and locations mentioned either are created to help inspire the story
or are real and used in a fictitious manner.

Cover Designer: Amanda Siegrist
Photos Provided by Evgeny Dubinchuk/kiuikson/Shutterstock.com
Edited by: Editing Done Write

Also By Amanda Siegrist

*A happy ending is all I need.*

**Consequences Novel**

Dark Consequences

Cruel Consequences

Fatal Consequences

**Haunting Love Novel**

Third Time's the Charm

Thirteen Days Gone

One Mistake Too Late

**Holiday Romance Novel**

Merry Me

Mistletoe Magic

Christmas Wish

Snowed in Love

Snowflakes and Shots

Holiday Hope

Sleigh All the Way

**Lucky Town Novel**

Escaping Memories

Dangerous Memories

Stolen Memories

Deadly Memories

Forgotten Memories

**McCord Family Novel**

Protecting You

Trust in Love

Deserving You

Always Kind of Love

Finding You

Dare You to Love

**Mona & Mason**

The Paranormal Chronicles, Volume I

**Perfect For You Novel**

The Wrong Brother

The Right Time

The Easy Part

The Hard Choice

**Psychic Love Novel**

Exploding Love

Captured Love

**Slaying Love Novel**

Won't Let You Go

Doomed Love

Deadly Crazy

Evidence of Sin

Finding Redemption

Obsessed Hope

# 1

UGH, not again.

Always a bridesmaid, never a bride.

That saying gets so old. Why did people insist on saying that to her? Because she might actually freak out one of these times.

"Doesn't that hurt your feelings, dear?" Lily's Aunt Zenda said as Sarafina stared at her with a smile. Having no smile would just bring more disastrous questions.

"When are you going to find yourself a handsome man?" Aunt Zenda said without waiting for a reply.

Darnation. Maybe her smile wasn't bright enough. Here was her chance to freak out. She'd had enough.

"I'm just waiting for the perfect man like you found with Henry." She couldn't freak out on Lily's aunt. Definitely the wrong person to do that to, but she could switch the conversation with ease. Butter her up with compliments about her own marriage, or anything that had to do with her in general, and she changed course as fast as a NASCAR pit crew changed tires.

"Oh, you are so right, dear. Why Henry, just the other day, he did the sweetest thing..."

Did she care what Henry did? No. Absolutely not. That simply reinforced all the good ones were taken. *When are you going to find yourself a handsome man*? Jeepers, if only she could've answered with, "As soon as all the men stop acting like bottom-feeding tadpoles and act like a true gentleman."

Of course, that would've opened a series of questions she didn't want to answer. What did she mean by that? "Oh, you poor thing, did some man break your heart?"

You poor thing. Goodness, she hated hearing that as much as the other dratted saying—always a bridesmaid. Maybe she wasn't as lucky as she could be in the man department. Sure, she had her heart broken a time or two. But all the good ones were snatched away before she had a chance to throw a sweet smile their way.

"...and then he came home with flowers. Isn't that the sweetest thing? The entire day was simply wonderful," Aunt Zenda said with a laugh.

Sarafina nodded, the same permanent smile on her face, because she had no clue what story Aunt Zenda delivered. Her mind derailed like it always did when she talked to her. "Henry's something else. You know—"

"I do know, dear. I was hoping you'd bring him up. Travis is perfect for you. You're walking down the aisle with him, aren't you?"

Her smile dipped. Just a fraction. She had a lifetime of how to perfect acting with Lily's family. But this question threw her off a little. Travis? Lily's brother? A big fat no. He was nothing more than a big brother to her.

"I'm not. I'm walking down with...ah...one of Ryan's friends. I haven't met him yet. I should really go check on

Lily. It was so nice to catch up, Aunt Zenda. Let's talk more later."

"Yes, dear, always a pleasure. Chin up. Your day's coming." Aunt Zenda frowned and patted her shoulder in reassurance.

One nod and a smile. Horrible conversation over.

Sometimes, it didn't pay to respond. Especially when she hadn't been feeling down about this wedding. Heavens no. Lily was her best friend. Nothing but excitement raced through her veins. Until she ran into someone like Aunt Zenda. She probably wouldn't be the only one to say that dreaded saying. There was nothing wrong with being a bridesmaid. All. The. Time. Nothing wrong whatsoever.

Aunt Zenda was right, of course. She was *always* the bridesmaid. Half of her friends were already married, with nearly the other half engaged. Because she was close with everyone, always the friendly one, the generous one, the go-to gal if you needed anything, she was always asked to be a bridesmaid.

Anytime a friend asked, she gladly accepted the humble responsibility, never taking a moment of it for granted. She considered it an honor to be asked. A true honor. She cherished each moment, each wedding as if it were the first time she was asked.

But a girl could only take so much, especially with the constant chatter and annoying statements thrown at her recently.

She paused mid-step as she walked down the church hallway. Oh, jeepers.

The dating game.

Was it time to get back into the dating game? Not that she stopped trying. Certainly not. She merely hadn't gone out of her way to snag a new man. Perhaps now would be a good time.

She continued walking.

Not at the wedding, of course. After. She'd find a great man after the wedding. No matter how hard it would be, she'd stick to her checklist. The perfect kind of man she wanted. Her very own Prince Charming. In the correct order, too. No skipping this time.

Kind. Check one.

Funny. Check two.

Thoughtful. Check three.

Good in bed. Check four.

Okay. Maybe she should move that last one up a few slots. Check one?

Nope. That needed to stay on the bottom. Where had it gotten her already? Nowhere. That's where.

Every time she tried the dating game, hunting for a man who would be perfect for her, she failed in every aspect. She always thought she snagged a prime catch, reeling that sucker in like she'd won a fishing contest.

First, there was Bradley. Delicious in bed. He topped 'good in bed' without breaking a sweat. First-prize winner every time. That should've been her huge warning sign. He didn't make it much farther down the list. He cheated on her with his secretary.

Then came Todd. He didn't even make it past check one when she brought him to a family gathering and he made her six-year-old cousin, who had a speech impediment, feel like it was something to be ashamed of. He even had the audacity to mock her cousin in front of her after they left the party. She never had the temptation to hit someone before, but that time it almost consumed her. Instead, she hopped out of his car before he could back out of the driveway and told him he better leave before her brother came out with his baseball bat. He was gone in under two seconds.

Her favorite one. Dominic. He made it far on the checklist, plus some. He had been her true love. Her one and only. Her soul mate. Her cosmic power that centered her world daily. That was, until he cheated on her.

She would like to say it broke her heart, but in truth, it had set her free. He hadn't really cheated on her, per se, like Bradley had. He had the decency to let her down gently that it wasn't going to work between them before he took the plunge with another person.

But she had felt stripped of something magical, something special, something that all her other friends had. To this day, he was still her one and only...best friend.

His new relationship was doing great. She couldn't be happier for him. Truly, unconditionally happy. Considering he was gay and couldn't continue to ignore that, she was more than glad he found happiness. Just not at times when the reminder she was alone and still hearing those dratted words from people like Aunt Zenda.

A spa session and maybe even a makeover with Dominic seemed crucial. And his partner, Freddy, well, he was the master makeover king if she ever saw one. He could take the most bedraggled human being and turn them into the most gorgeous creature living on the planet. She wasn't calling herself ugly, but sometimes a girl needed a little sprucing up to gain some happiness back. To know that she was a worthy catch.

The minute she saw Dominic, she'd tell him to schedule an appointment with Freddy for her. She could already hear him saying, "Darling, you don't need to see Freddy with an appointment. He'll get you in on the spot. He'll drop anyone for you." She knew he would, too, but his time was precious and deserved respect. She would, of course, argue with Dominic until she got her way. A pure master. He could never win an argument with her, no matter the issue. Well, besides the one where he wasn't really gay. She had talked herself blue on that one. Perhaps she should call him now. If she didn't tell him right away, she might lose her nerve to go through with it.

Patting the sides of her dress, she muttered under her breath. So much for letting Dominic know right away. No pockets. Duh. She left her phone in the room where Lily was beautifying herself. Her best friend, Lily, was finally getting married. It still seemed surreal at times.

While she thought of Dominic as her best friend—her guy best friend—Lily was her girl best friend. Some days, she didn't know how she would've survived the aftermath of Dominic telling her he was gay if Lily hadn't been there.

She had hoped to be her maid of honor. Sometimes, it felt like a nasty fate bestowed upon her always asked to be in her friends' weddings as a bridesmaid, but she was never the maid of honor. Only a simple bridesmaid. Just once, she would like to be a maid of honor. Or the bride. That would be lovely, too. To have her own fairytale romance. Only in her dreams, apparently.

She had been totally let down and disappointed. Silly to feel that way. She knew Lily's family well. So well, she was practically considered one of their daughters. But when it came to family, Lily never disobeyed. Her mother had immediately said her sister would be her maid of honor without asking or batting an eye toward Lily. It was said with simple authority. One thing a person never did was disobey or question the words of her mother, and especially her father.

Lily had smiled at her mother and nodded enthusiastically. Of course, when they left the house—because yes, she had been there when it happened—Lily apologized profusely.

"I'm sorry, Fina. I was going to ask you. I truly was. I didn't expect my mother to say that at all. She knows Lora and I don't get along."

"She's your sister. I understand. Don't worry, Lily. I know when your mother says something, it's like it's written in gold."

"But you'll be one of my bridesmaids, right? Say you will."

"It would be my honor."

A real honor. This wedding, out of every wedding she had been a part of, was a true honor. She would do anything for Lily. Absolutely anything. She was her best friend.

Finding her right now and making sure pre-jitter nerves weren't swarming her body, she figured it was a good time to quit wallowing in self-pity. For the day, anyway. Tomorrow she would pick up where her mind had wandered and enter pity-land. Sometimes, a girl had to pull that gallon of ice cream out and eat her pity away. She would do that, then call Dominic for an appointment with Freddy. Purge herself of all that sadness and find a new man. It was time she became the bride for once.

Deep breath. She would survive the day.

Running her hands down the soft contours of her periwinkle dress, she released one more breath.

No need to be nervous. She had done this a million times already. Nothing new. She couldn't remember exactly how many times she had been a bridesmaid.

Seven times. No. Probably more like ten. Maybe this one made it eleven. Or was it nine?

Did it truly matter? Nope.

She loved this dress. Loved it. Lily made sure she picked a dress that complemented her. Of course, no matter how many times she walked down the aisle as a bridesmaid, she always managed to look elegant and beautiful. Not as gorgeous as the bride, but she held her own. That alone made her nervous when her day finally came, making her think she wouldn't look as elegant and beautiful.

Utterly silly. Of course, she would look elegant and beautiful. Her wedding day would be the grandest day of her life. She would look like a princess, feel like one, and be the most cherished woman on earth by the true love of her life. Whoever that fellow might be. She would hopefully know soon after Freddy used his magic hands with her hair.

"Oh, jeepers, I'm so sorry," she mumbled, trailing her eyes up a broad chest to a face she didn't recognize. And she would've recognized him if she had seen him before. His bright-green eyes twinkled, a slight amusement lingering. This wasn't the time to be running into handsome men. She needed all her wits about her. Running into handsome men was supposed to come after the wedding, not before.

"My fault. I wasn't paying attention." He offered a charming smile, lighting his eyes up even more as he let his hands drop from her shoulders. "I'm Dax. I'm sorry for almost knocking you down."

He reached out his hand. She couldn't possibly shake his hand. The brief moment when she smacked her face into his chest, his hands grabbing her to steady her, sent a small tingling flame of desire down the length of her body. So brief, her imagination had probably simply run away from her. A simple touch couldn't possibly send a burst of pleasure that quickly. What would it feel like to hold his hand?

His brow rose at her lack of response. Oh geez, she was

acting like an idiot. She shoved her hand into his. "I'm Fina... or Sarafina. Most people call me Fina. You can call me that. Or you can call me Sarafina. Heck, some people even call me Sara." She cleared her throat. She did not just ramble like that. Since when did she ramble like a moron? How long would he continue to hold her hand? Those flames of desire were starting to burn her from the inside out. Her imagination was intact. The tingles were real. And very, very wonderful.

He caressed her hand with the tip of his thumb before letting her go. "It's a pleasure to meet you, Sarafina. You have a beautiful name. Are you a bridesmaid?" He glanced at her dress, a small laugh escaping. "Of course, you are. What position are you walking down?"

A trembling hand slid down her dress. "Um...I'm third. Why?"

Her insides continued to melt when another laugh left his mouth. "Me, too. It'll be my pleasure to escort you down the aisle."

Pleasure. Yeah, she was feeling plenty of that. *Keep the smile. Do not look terrified at that prospect.* How would she manage down the aisle with his warm hand on her the entire time? "Great. You weren't at the rehearsal dinner, were you?"

"No, I had some business I needed to wrap up. Are you a friend or family of the bride?"

"A friend. You?"

"I went to college with Ryan."

They stared at each other. She wanted to say it unnerved her, but she was almost getting used to the way his eyes held hers. Mesmerized. Enchanted.

*Pathetic, Sarafina.* Oh darnation. This was too much. His gorgeous smile indicated he wanted to say more. But they had nothing else to say. Unless to brainstorm where the nearest closet could be found.

Nope. Bad idea. Not happening.

She needed some air. Especially if his hands would be touching her again so soon.

"I need a last-minute touch-up...and I should go see if Lily needs my help. I'll see you soon," she said a bit awkwardly.

"I can't wait."

---

DAX WATCHED as she hustled away, hiking her dress up a little. It gave him a lovely view of her legs. Way too lovely of legs.

Screwed. Easiest way to put it. This would be a lot harder than he imagined.

He groaned as she disappeared around the corner. How did he always manage to get involved in bad situations? Worst decision ever. He jumped slightly when a hand grabbed his shoulder.

"I really wish you'd stick by me," Ryan said, the annoyance plain in his tone.

Dax resisted the urge to roll his eyes. "I'm a big boy. I don't need a baby-sitter. I was meeting the lovely Sarafina who I'll be walking down the aisle."

"Keep your damn hands to yourself. I don't need any trouble. I don't want this," Ryan said through clenched teeth.

"You have no say. You're the one who decided to marry a woman who has ties to the Chilani family. Let me do my job. Go fix your bow tie. I'll be right there."

"If you ruin my wedding, I'll..." Ryan shook his head and walked away.

"Good choice, buddy, not finishing that sentence," Dax muttered under his breath.

Damn this assignment. He never worked undercover. Or had such a quick reaction to a woman before. Honey-golden hair. Hazel eyes. Softest skin imaginable. He needed to get Sarafina out of his head. Focus on the job. Definitely, worst decision ever.

He could honestly say it wouldn't be a hardship escorting the lovely Sarafina down the aisle. The hard part would be keeping his hands to himself. She had sparked a desire by one simple bump. He couldn't imagine what holding her as they walked down the aisle, maybe even sharing a dance or two at the reception, would do to his libido.

It had been a while. Or, more like, too long since he had a woman. Just the way he liked it. After the fiasco with his ex, Bridget, he didn't want to deal with another woman. Too much work. He already had enough real work to deal with. He didn't need a nagging, in-your-face, why-don't-you-ever-have-time-for-me woman again. Because that's all he ever heard from Bridget.

"You're never around, Dax. All you do is work, work, work. What about me? What about my feelings?"

He wanted to say, "What about me? I saw you flirting with my partner, Colt, just last week." But pointing that out would've started a new slew of accusations from her that he didn't want to hear. So he simply nodded his head, like 'yeah, I work too much.' Sometimes, it was better to agree with a woman than to argue.

Unfortunately, that sentiment and way of thinking had made him a single man. Bridget moved out not long after.

Her parting words, "You never communicate. I can't stand the silence from you."

For him, silence was golden. He liked the silence. Appreciated it. Very, very fond of it. Most days, anyway. Some days. Very rare days. He didn't like the silence so much. On those occasions, he did what he did best: worked.

For the first time in his life, he hated his work. Normally, his job was his livelihood. Today, more like a form of torture. Just thinking about escorting Sarafina down the aisle had his skin prickling with delightful goose bumps. His hands itched to touch her again. Such beauty.

No touching.

He needed to remember that. Of course, sure, he had to touch her while he walked down the aisle. But after that, definitely no touching. Hands away, tucked nicely in his pockets.

Making his way back to Ryan, he tried to forget why he was here. Not that it did him any good. He could still hear his boss's voice ringing in his ear.

"You're our man, Dax. The show is yours."

"Come on, Sloan. Don't ask me to do this. That man was a good friend of mine in college. I can't betray his trust like this."

"That's the only reason I'm asking you to do this, *because* he was a good friend of yours in college. We can't tip off Martin Chilani that we're putting an FBI agent in his daughter's wedding. This is serious, Dax. One tip-off that you're an agent and you're a dead man. He will get rid of you so fast, you won't even know it's happening. We don't have time to get another agent ready for this undercover op and make a story seem believable. You were good friends with the groom in college. Nobody in the family will suspect a thing."

"And they won't do a background check on me? It'll be pretty simple to see I work for the FBI."

"Your friend, Ryan, never knew you went into the academy. You fell out of touch with him before you did. All he knows is you majored in business. That's the cover we'll create. That'll be easier to create than sending in somebody else." Supervisor Special Agent Rick Sloan had leaned forward, cradling his hands into a tight ball over his desk. "Look, Dax, I know I'm asking for a lot. I also know you're betraying a friendship, but the Chilanis have been causing too much havoc. We know there is a fresh shipment of weapons coming into the city, and we need to waylay that shipment. The tip we got is good intel. We need you to get a little closer to find the exact location."

"What makes you think Ryan will know anything?"

Sloan had thrown his hands up. "I don't know that he will know anything. But you'll be surrounded at his wedding by the Chilani family. Maybe you'll hear something you shouldn't. We have to take this opportunity. You're a damn fine agent. You can do this."

Yeah, right. He was starting to think he really couldn't do this. Right from the start, it had been complete shit. They pulled Ryan off the street, explaining in detail what would happen, and Ryan had immediately glared daggers at him as if he were the lowest scum of the earth. At times, he felt like it.

Refusing to cooperate at first, he had to watch as his supervisor threatened to lock up Ryan and his fiancée for any small thing he could think of. He threatened the part about his fiancée a little more than Dax had appreciated. Ryan had sat in the chair, ticking like a time bomb, his rage for the treatment about his fiancée clear.

Even after he got Ryan alone to explain everything in

better terms, nothing would penetrate Ryan's thick skull to make him feel better. Dax figured all he could think about was the threat against his fiancée.

Part of Ryan's reluctance made Dax wonder if maybe he knew more than he wanted to admit. Did Ryan even know what sort of family he was marrying into? He hadn't appeared too surprised when they went down the list of transgressions that Martin Chilani committed. That was the worst part that concerned Dax.

His friend—very good friend from his college days—was beyond pissed off with him. Was he so upset that he would blow Dax's cover?

The only safe answer could be no. Otherwise, Dax would be six feet under the minute it happened. He knew this. He tried to mentally prepare for it. But how could one prepare to die cruelly? And cruel it would be. He saw many reports of the crimes Martin Chilani was accused of.

Accused being the operative word. They could never get anything to stick in court, no matter how hard they tried. So any time they got a decent, reliable tip to bring down Martin Chilani, they took advantage of the opportunity.

Dax wished this time it wouldn't have screwed with his life.

No sweat. Just another assignment. He had wanted to check the perimeter before the wedding, eye the guests arriving, but now he knew he needed to get back to Ryan.

Sarafina had derailed his plans. Not a good sign. Already finding a distraction. An unwanted distraction. He needed to focus his mind on the job, not on a woman. Definitely not on a woman. They were nothing but trouble.

Dax walked into the small room in the bottom of the church and found Ryan alone, staring intensely into a mirror on the wall. Ryan looked at him through the mirror, his expression not giving him any happy vibes.

"Do you want me to say I'm sorry again? I don't want this just as much as you."

"I doubt that. I love Lily. I love everything about her. This day is supposed to be the best day of her life."

Dax took a step toward him, the sincerity as prominent as he could make it. "It will be. I'm not here to ruin your wedding."

Ryan turned around, his fists clenched by his sides. "No, you're here to arrest her father."

"Did you not hear anything we told you? Murder, extortion, bribery, drug distribution, weapon charges. Just the icing on the cake. He's capable of so much more. Or perhaps you already know all of this and it just doesn't affect you."

"He's never been convicted of a crime. Innocent until proven guilty. Isn't that how the law works, Dax? I mean, you should know, since you're the law."

"I'm good at my job. I won't justify my reasons and actions to you. Care to know some of the reasons he's never been convicted before?"

Ryan swiveled back toward the mirror with his head down. "I thought I knew you. You were supposed to be my friend."

Dax almost took another step toward him, but stopped. Getting into a fight with the groom right before the ceremony wouldn't go over well with any member of the Chilani family, or his boss.

"I am your friend. Because I'm your friend, I'm trying to help you as well. I know you love her. But at least you're properly informed what kind of man her father is. One wrong move toward his daughter...what do you think he'll do to you?"

Ryan's eyes lifted, flickering an intense emotion before clouding over, masking any emotion. "Just curious. What would you've done if one of my groomsmen hadn't had that accident and broken his leg? Part of me wonders if it really was an accident. It makes a man curious how I suddenly needed another groomsman a few days before my wedding, and I get picked up by the FBI telling me that I don't have to worry about finding a new grooms-man. They have one for me. I don't like lying to my fiancée."

"And I don't want to be six feet under the ground. You tell her anything and I'm a dead man. Is that what you want, Ryan?" Clenching his jaw to avoid spewing more words that would cause even more of a bridge between them, he took a step back. "We had nothing to do with your friend breaking his leg. I had nothing to do with that. Everything just fell into place. That's why we don't want to pass up this opportu-nity. I can only say I'm sorry."

"I don't want your damn apologies anymore. I won't leak your dirty secret because, with everything you told me, if I choose to believe it, how do I know Mr. Chilani won't blame me, too?"

"You don't know. And I would say he would."

"Your secret's safe with me." He looked down, rubbing his wrist as he glanced at his watch. "I'm about to get married. Get the hell out, Dax. I need a moment."

What else could he say? Nothing. Absolutely nothing would make him feel better.

Closing the door behind him, Dax made his way to his original destination. The front of the church. He wanted to see who was arriving, who was already in attendance. Hone in on conversations. Catch any whispering words was his goal. He needed the information he came for and then he would get the hell out of Dodge. After the wedding, of course.

Unless he wanted to join witness protection, his cover needed to stay intact, even after any arrests were made. Martin Chilani could never know the leak came from him or Ryan. He knew his friend appeared to hate him at the moment, but he'd still protect Ryan with his life. If Martin Chilani got so much as a whiff that Ryan was involved, he would be a dead man. Married to his daughter or not. Dead man. Dax hoped Ryan fully understood that.

Dax turned the corner and collided with a warm, soft body, and grabbed ahold of Sarafina once again. This time, not letting go as quickly as the first time.

"We have to quit running into each other. Maybe we should practice walking side by side so we don't screw up the walk down the aisle," he said with a grin that normally had women melting at his feet. To his great relief, her smile widened even further.

"I've been down the aisle so many times, I can't screw it up. As long as you hold onto me tightly, you'll be safe in my arms."

"Isn't that my line? I'm supposed to keep you safe in *my* arms. How many times did you practice walking down the aisle last night? Now I feel terrible for not making it."

She shivered, whether from his words or from his touch, he wasn't sure. It was enough of a sign that he dropped his hands and backed up a step. The strength it took to do that surprised him.

"We didn't practice that long. I've been a bridesmaid quite a lot. I feel like a pro." She laughed nervously, running her hands down her dress, then pointed an accusing finger at him. "And don't you dare say it."

He held his hands up in an innocent gesture. "I won't, I

swear." Then he leaned forward with a sly smile. "What am I not supposed to say?"

She giggled, shoving his hands down with a playful push. "You know, the line. Always a bridesmaid..."

"Ah...and you're never a bride." He gave her a sheepish grin. "I said half of it. Am I in the doghouse now?"

Every time she laughed or smiled, he mentally prepared how to make her do it again. Her sweet disposition brightened his mood more than anything else could.

"No, I suppose not. Do I have to worry about you running into me again later? I want to prepare myself."

He laughed. Damn, she had a wonderful, witty humor. What a refreshing encounter compared with other women he dated. Not that he wanted to date her. "I would have to say you ran into me both times. Do *I* have to worry about it?"

"A gentleman would never blame the woman," she said, raising a brow for him to counter that with as much flare as she gave.

He leaned closer, his lips brushing her ear as he whispered, "I'm not always a gentleman, but for you, I shall try not to run into you again."

Before the temptation to kiss her neck, peppering a small trail to her lips, came over him, he pulled away. "Shall we practice walking down the aisle?"

He offered his arm. He wanted her to touch him, and that was so wrong on so many levels.

No touching.

But the minute she looped her arm through his, he couldn't even remember his name. The only thing that mattered was the beautiful woman next to him and how he never wanted to let go.

## 2

SARAFINA TRIED NOT to shake from the pulsing ache that wouldn't go away. A simple loop of his arm and hand lightly covering hers was making her sweat with desire. She could only imagine what it would feel like for him to really *touch* her.

Chancing a glance out of the corner of her eye, she inspected his features a little more. He was delicious to look at. Probably even more delicious to taste.

*Get your head out of the gutter, Sarafina.*

He had brown hair, slightly on the long side, that he combed back stylishly with a smooth curl. It made him appear boyish in a way, yet sexy. Like a sweet but *very* sexy boy next door. It would be better for her if she didn't think that way. That would only lead her straight into trouble. Because Dax looked like trouble with a capital T, regardless of his boyish looks. Even his name sounded like trouble.

Unable to explain why she thought that, but knowing deep down in the pit of her stomach he was, she wrapped her heart in another protective layer. She would wait to find a new man until after the wedding. Dax wasn't stepping into that role, no matter how much the idea enticed her.

Her eyes continued their path down his jawline, fascinated by the sharp contours of his face. So kissable.

*For heaven sakes, you are not kissing the man, even if he has a kissable face.*

"Are you okay?" a soft voice whispered in her ear, sending another bout of anticipating shivers throughout her body.

"Of course. Why wouldn't I be?"

"You're shaking. Did you have breakfast? I know weddings can get crazy, but I hope you managed to grab a bite to eat. It's not good to have an empty stomach."

She turned her head a little, figuring that would be better than his hot breath continually rushing down her body every time a word left his mouth. Boy, she was wrong. The concern sparkling in his eyes almost had her dropping to the floor in a puddle of goo.

"I had breakfast. It's cold in here. I think they have the air-conditioning blasted on high."

He let go of her arm, briefly rubbing both of her arms up and down. That thick layer of protection to cloak her heart shook a little, crumbling a tiny corner off.

"How's that? I'd give you my jacket, but considering it's almost our turn to walk down the aisle, I don't think everyone else would appreciate that."

"Much better. Thank you." She looped her arm through his again, leaning into him. "Are you ready? You were a pro at our practice session."

The smile that lit up his face was enough to heat her body to an inferno. Maybe they needed to turn the air-conditioner a little lower.

"I appreciate you teaching me the finer techniques of walking down the aisle. I know I'm safe in your arms."

She giggled. "I thought that you were supposed to say that I'm safe in your arms."

"Turns out I might like being saved by a woman for once. At least, if that woman is you." His head moved closer to her neck, his mouth brushing her ear. "How about we save each other? I sense you don't want to particularly do this again. And I hate having eyes on me. In a way, we're saving each other."

How did she respond to those daring words? Because he had her pegged to a T. She didn't want to do this again. For Lily, of course, she would, but she was getting sick of walking down the aisle as a bridesmaid. It would be wonderful to attend a wedding for once as a simple guest, or as the darn bride.

Saved from having to answer with another, hopefully, witty response, Clara, the wedding planner, swept by them, whispering, "It's time, people. On my count. One. Two. Three." And with a point of her finger, she gestured for them to start walking.

Dax took control easily, leading her down the aisle. A genuine smile formed, because no matter how much she dreaded doing this once again, she was truly happy for Lily.

Dax smiled just as brightly next to her, his eyes centered ahead, looking at his friend Ryan. She thought she saw a flash of anger come from Ryan, a tense movement from Dax, but dismissed it quickly when Ryan's smile never wavered. Perhaps she misinterpreted what she saw.

Nerves. Everyone had nerves when it came to a wedding. She had an entire bundle of nerves to contend with.

And to her mortification, after teasing Dax relentlessly that she would save him down the aisle, he was the one who saved her. Halfway down the trek, her eyes met Franklin, Lily's annoying cousin, making her trip on her feet.

Dax's steady arm held her upright, not even missing a beat. Her face, poised with a smile no matter how tense she became, never indicated that she almost tumbled to the ground. Dax had fluidly kept her upright and stable as if nothing even happened.

Although her body tingled with frightened goose bumps as she could feel Franklin's eyes on her the entire time, Dax kept her sane and in control. She knew he sensed her discomfort, probably aching to ask her what the problem was, but ever the gentleman he claimed he wasn't, he continued down the path with grace, her hanging on his arm like a prized jewel.

That's exactly how she felt, too, holding his arm. A prized jewel. And not just any savory jewel, but his. Only his. That simple thought had her forgetting about Franklin's unnerving stare and continuing to her spot at the head of the church without further incident.

The ceremony continued at a delicate pace, Lily the center of attention the entire time, as she should be. Although her eyes were glued to the happy couple standing in front of her, she occasionally peeked a glance or two at Dax, always seeing him eye her back.

One sultry glance here. Another heated glance there. She burned with desire every time his eyes landed on her. Perhaps knowing the effect he had on her, his lips always curled with devilish delight, exciting her even further.

Before long, the ceremony was finished. As natural as could be, she looped her arm through his and let him escort her back down the aisle. To have him holding her, yet again, was pure heaven. She wanted to fling hateful accusations everywhere that the show was over. Walking down the aisle hadn't been so bad with him by her side. She wanted to walk that same path a few more times just to imprint the memory firmly into her brain. Maybe even let a few tears escape that the walk down the aisle was officially over.

"Save a dance for me, Sarafina. I enjoy you in my arms."

Her body trembled with longing as his whispered words floated around her, cocooning her into a happy place that she hadn't experienced in such a long time. With a parting smile as he walked away and joined the other groomsmen, she wondered if she imagined his sweet words. He didn't even wait for her response.

Wanting Dax was a very bad thing.

"Oh my God! Fina, I'm a married woman. I feel like fainting," Lily exclaimed as she grabbed a tight hug from her.

"Oh, jeepers. If that was going to happen, you would've done that already. It was all so beautiful." Sarafina hugged Lily back, almost crying from the happiness she had for her friend.

"You're right, of course. Now the real party starts. Ryan and I will be in the first limo. Ryan gave me a look like he wanted to ravish me silly already."

Sarafina giggled with her, picturing what Ryan had in mind for the ride to the reception. "Well, enjoy. You deserve it."

"You enjoy as well." Lily winked naughtily.

"What does that mean?"

"Please, girl. I might be focused on my wedding, but I'm not blind when my best friend is eyeing a very fine man."

"Ryan is waiting for you." Sarafina pointed behind her as she tried to ignore the ridiculous grin on her face. "I have no idea what you're talking about."

Lily pulled her in for another hug. "I believe his name is

Dax and he's Ryan's friend. He's hot. You're single. So is he. That's all I'm saying. Go for it."

Sarafina laughed as Lily waggled her eyebrows with playfulness, hiked up her massive dress, and ran to Ryan with a joyful smile.

He's single. How in the world did Lily know that? Leave it to Lily to lay it straight. Could it really hurt to take a chance? She had originally planned to find a man after the wedding. Perhaps her plans could be rearranged. Seems she already found a man. He was sweet, sexy, and currently single. And he already reserved a dance with her. What more could she ask for?

Linking arms with Lily's sister, Lora, as she came up next to her with excitement, they made their way to the second limo. Although, Lily and Lora didn't particularly get along all the time, Sarafina had no such trouble. She normally got along with everyone.

"Mastered that walk down the aisle once again, Fina," Lora said with friendly delight. Although, Sarafina heard the mockery laced within.

"Easy-peasy. You look absolutely gorgeous, by the way. I can feel my hair drooping from the humidity already and you're still looking like a queen."

Lora waved her hand frivolously in the air. "Please. You're too kind. You look gorgeous as well. Look at the hot man eyeing you. I kinda wished he had been the best man. I want to hang off his arm."

Sarafina followed Lora's eyes where they trained on Dax. He was looking their way, eyeing them both with a heated stare. Or was that stare exclusively for her? The way Lora said it, he was staring at her. Could she truly be that lucky?

"He's very nice."

Lora scoffed. "Nice? Fina, you need to stop doing nice.

Where has that gotten you? Nowhere, that's where. I think it's time you did something dirty. Because if you're not..."

Sarafina flashed her eyes to Lora, hearing the unspoken words clear as day. "Are you asking for permission to make a move on him? I have no claim on the man."

"Perhaps not, but you were paired with him. Douglas, Ryan's best man, is already married. Not that I can't go there, but I don't really feel like ruining a marriage today. Dax looks like a nice replacement. We don't really know anything about him. I love an air of mystery. Daddy wasn't too happy when Sean broke his leg and in popped this mystery man. If you were thinking about snagging him tonight, I'll back off. I might not even get that far with him. He seriously can't take his eyes off you."

Sarafina slowly turned her head toward him again, feeling the heated desire that poured from his eyes. A nice cold bucket of water would do her well right now. Lora had it right. He was looking at her.

"You know me, Lora. I'm not very aggressive with men or pick the right ones. You're free to snag him all you want."

Lora's eyes widened with mock surprise, knowing quite well Sarafina would never deny her the opportunity. "You're the best, Fina. Truly the best. I'll meet you in the limo. I have some snagging to do."

*Clink, clink, clink.* That armor around her heart was securely in place again. At least, that's what she tried to tell herself as Lora dropped her arm and beelined it to the limo where Dax stood with the other groomsmen.

Lying had never been a strong suit for her. Not that Lora could tell.

She wasn't aggressive when it came to men. Hadn't she already established that Dax was trouble? The best solution was to back off. Let Lora have a chance. Not to mention, saying no to Lora wouldn't go over well. Sarafina learned early in life, being friends with Lily, that Lora always got her way. Always.

One simple look toward her father, and whatever was denied swiftly turned in her favor. Not that she didn't get along with Mr. C. Untrue. He had told her more than once he considered her part of the family, almost like a daughter. But she had never been on the receiving end of his wrath. She certainly didn't want to tempt it now. Better to let Lora have her way.

She watched, somewhat painfully, as Lora slid up against Dax in a provocative manner. He didn't hesitate to slide his hand around her waist and then laughed at something she said.

Apparently, those heated glances hadn't been geared towards her after all. Turning away from the newly happy couple, she waved good-bye to Lily right before the driver shut the door to her limo. Making her way slowly to her own limo, she smiled politely as Douglas held the door open for her.

"Looking lovely today, Fina. I bet you'll be happy to get into some air-conditioning. I know this heat is killing me."

"I am, Douglas. It's getting hotter as the day progresses. You look quite dashing yourself. How's Cathy?"

"Most beautiful woman here." He leaned closer, laughing. "But don't let the bride hear that."

She chuckled. "She's your wife. Your secret is safe with me."

"We can always count on you to keep a secret." Douglas winked at her and kissed her cheek before she slid into the limo.

Being one of the last ones to enter the limo, she had no choice but to plant herself in the only spot available. Right next to Dax. He gave her a sultry smile as she slid next to him, her thigh touching his. As Douglas entered as the last person, she had no choice but to squeeze tighter next to Dax. Her entire body brushed up against his hard body. Oh, the shivering pleasure from that simple contact.

"Are you okay?" he whispered into her ear.

"I'm fine. Glad to be where the cool air is."

He nodded once, suddenly turning his attention to Lora as she demanded his attention. Sarafina, although not wanting to, kept a sweet smile on her face as they ventured to the reception.

Was she okay? Not really. Earlier, she had been looking forward to the reception, and now she dreaded it with every breath in her body as she listened to Dax and Lora laughing like old lovers.

Not okay at all.

**3**

SITTING NEXT to this woman and listening to her aggravating laugh was enough to want to put a bullet through his head. The minute Lora Chilani slid up to him, wrapping her arms around him, he knew he had a great opening into the affairs of the Chilani family. A quick glance at Sarafina had him hesitating, but only for a moment.

He was here to do a job, not fall in love. Sarafina did not register on his scale of priorities, even if he wanted to send her to the top.

Snuggling Lora closer to his body as he laughed at her flirting that did nothing for him, he reinforced the decision to do his job without further distractions.

Because that's what Sarafina was—a simple distraction. He couldn't afford even a small one. The tiniest distraction could get him killed. That was the last thing he wanted to do today. He wasn't ready to die.

But that damn distraction was sitting right next to him, bundled so close to his body, it was difficult not to turn and mold her more perfectly to his frame. And she smelled delicious. A sweet scent of vanilla and lavender. Perhaps her shampoo. Or maybe some sort of hairspray as her hair look coiled to perfection. Or his favorite, a lovely fragrance from a perfume bottle. He always loved a woman wearing a light, airy perfume that enticed him to come closer.

That's exactly what her scent was doing to him. He wanted to get so close it would be indecent in front of everyone.

"So, what do you do, Dax? With all the crazy details with the wedding, Ryan barely had a chance to tell us more about you," Lora crooned.

"Business. I work on Wall Street. The details are rather boring and tedious. I'd rather hear more about you." After speaking that lie, he touched the tip of her nose delicately as if he really wanted to know more about her.

Sarafina shivered next to him. Damn, was she still cold? It would be okay to give her his coat now, except he had this other horrid woman hanging off him. She was either cold, like she claimed before, or her body struggled to keep up with the craziness of the day. Did she really eat like she said she did?

*Focus. She is not your concern.*

"I would love to know more about you," Lora said in a delicate whisper as she almost pressed her entire body over his.

"Get a room, Lora. Leave the poor man alone, at least while we're in the vehicle with you," Jane yelled from the other end of the limo.

"Screw you, Jane," Lora replied.

"If you swing that way, honey, I'm game," Jane said with a seductive smirk.

The entire limo roared with laughter, even Lora, who gave her an appreciative glance.

Now Dax wanted to shiver. With disgust. He had the

distinct impression that Lora would take her up on the offer, then jump into bed with a man. What in the hell was he getting himself into? It was like playing with fire and getting blown to bits before the flames even touched him.

Twenty excruciating minutes later, they made it to the reception hall at one of the most luxurious hotels in New York City. Even Dax had to admit he was impressed and looking forward to seeing the inside. Elegance gleamed from the windows to the debonair doorman standing outside.

Sarafina obviously exited before him, making him want to groan with longing as he watched her butt sway away, trying to reel him in. Ignoring the temptation walking away, he exited the limo and then turned around, holding his hand out for Lora.

"You are such a gentleman."

He smiled, unsure of what flirty thing to say. Sarafina's delectable body wouldn't disappear from his mind.

"Daddy, have you met Dax yet?"

Dax whipped his head to his left where Martin Chilani approached from the vehicle behind theirs. The man could stop the entire New York City traffic in its tracks. Authority, power, and a sense of intellect exuded from him in waves.

Black hair with some gray sprinkled in gave him almost a young, grandfatherly look. Eyes of gold that spoke of intelligence and an awareness that he knew what you were thinking. And his state of dress, pressed, wrinkle-free, as if he hadn't taken a twenty-minute drive like the rest of them.

The man scared the shit out of Dax. And not much scared him.

"I don't believe I have yet, princess," Mr. Chilani said with tenderness, then trained his eyes directly at Dax. The stare unnerved him. "Daxton Delcroy. A pleasure to finally meet one of Ryan's good friends. From his college days, yes?"

Without showing an ounce of fear, Dax shook hands with the man, maintaining a firm grip. A notch of respect inched higher from Mr. Chilani by that simple feat. He could see it in his eyes. "Yes, old college roommates. It was great to hear from him after so long."

"And why such the long separation?"

"Sometimes life takes you places you didn't realize you'd go, and suddenly it's almost passed you by, making you wonder where the time went. I bet you can still remember when Lily was just a baby, and now she's a married woman. Time flies, sir."

Mr. Chilani laughed jovially. "It sure does. I'm still recovering from her getting married. Ryan is a good man. He'll treat her right."

Dax heard the silent *or else* as clear as the sunny blue sky.

"What do you do, Mr. Delcroy?"

"Please, Mr. Chilani, call me Dax. I work in the finance world. I—"

"On Wall Street, Daddy," Lora chimed in, like it was the most dazzling job in the world.

"Wall Street. Making some decent money then. What sort of finance?"

Dax tried not to lift his hand to loosen his bow tie from the sudden interrogation. He couldn't screw this up. Dead man, or still a groomsman of the wedding? Those were his only two outcomes.

"Stocks and bonds. A demanding, yet rewarding job. Money is always a pretty sight to see."

"Do you know Richard Tilleti?"

Oh, shit. Martin Chilani had done his homework on Dax immediately, already trying to test his cover story.

"Small world. That's my boss. Great man, difficult to please at times, but a generous boss."

"Oh, yes, he can be a difficult man." Mr. Chilani's eyes trailed to the building where Lily and Ryan were making their entrance. "I do believe the bride and groom have arrived. I look forward to sharing more stories with you about Richard. I never miss a chance to talk business."

Dax smiled, yet his insides tensed like a coiled snake. "I look forward to it."

"We shall see you inside then. Lora, a word with you."

Lora's face fell into a frown, her posture indicating the actions of a petulant child not getting their way. Dax gave her a friendly smile, nodded at Mr. Chilani, and walked away unscathed. For now, anyway.

Dax entered the plush hotel, following the throng of guests to the required destination, until Ryan suddenly appeared next to him with Lily holding his hand.

"Meeting the father of the bride. Not too bad, I hope," Ryan said with an underlying tension.

"Oh, stop, Ryan. I know my father can be intimidating, but he's not that bad." Lily slapped his arm, giving Dax a sincere smile.

"Just a friendly hello. Congratulations, Lily. You make Ryan one of the happiest men in the world. And you look beautiful."

She blushed at his words, surprising Dax. He would've thought she'd be used to compliments like that.

"Thank you. Let me be frank. Can I be forward with you?" She leaned closer as she said it.

"Of course." Dax leaned forward as well. What in the world did she want to be honest about?

"My sister is...not the brightest choice to pick. Perhaps someone more sweet, kind, and hasn't slept with half the population of New York would be better for you."

Ryan grimaced, hugging Lily closer to him. "Lily, Dax isn't looking for a woman tonight, are you, buddy?"

"No."

Lily rolled her eyes at Ryan. "Sweetie, it's a wedding. Things happen. I'm just trying to say, because I saw you standing by my sister, she's the wrong choice. I'm looking out for you. And I know you're probably thinking, well, that's your sister. Trust me when I say we're not close. If I would've had my way, Fina would've been my maid of honor, not Lora."

Ryan cleared his throat. "Probably not the best place to talk about that, honey. If your mother heard, well, that wouldn't end well. We both know you wanted Fina next to you. Plus, Dax isn't setting his sights on your sister...or Fina. Right, buddy?"

Dax tried not to cringe at the thought of Lora anywhere near him, or the sinking feeling that he shouldn't pursue Sarafina either. The thought hurt him more than he cared to admit.

"Right. Not in the market for a woman. Just enjoying the festivities. No worries about your sister. Look at it as me being polite and not wanting to hurt her feelings."

"Good. That makes me feel better." Lily turned her head to the right, her eyes widening with happiness. "Fina! Over here."

Dax sucked in a silent breath as the woman he wished to stay far away from walked their way. Begging his heart to slow down, he tipped his lips up into a gentle grin as she took a spot right next to him, Lily on her other side.

"Picture time. Who's ready for their face to fall off from

all the smiling about to happen?" Lily said with overexcitement. "So, you two stick close together. Because you have to stand next to your partner for the pictures. The. Entire. Time."

Those words vibrated through Dax's entire body. Could he handle that? He enjoyed holding Sarafina more than he should.

Sarafina slowly turned her head toward him, gingerly smiling. Unable to resist the potency of her smile, he matched her brightness with a smile of his own. Offering his arm, too far gone in the depths of her beauty, he needed to hold her once again.

"Shall we, partner? Standing for long periods of time with a smile on my face sounds like I require a bit of saving."

She looped her arm around his, nodding. "I think I can handle that. Although, I think you may be saving me this time. I hate taking pictures."

"Oh, she does. But you're gorgeous. Let's go. I want to start dancing soon," Lily said brightly as she shuffled Ryan away.

Dax didn't miss the level of warning coming from Ryan as he held on to Sarafina like he was drowning in the middle of the ocean.

"Are you still cold? I felt you shaking in the limo."

Her hazel eyes swallowed him whole as she swung her head from side to side. "I'm fine, honestly. Let's get this torture over with. Lily's not a huge fan of taking pictures either. Of course, for her wedding day, she'll suck it up, but she'll make this quick. Trust me."

"I do trust you, Sarafina."

*I also love being with you, touching you, and am dying to roam my hands in unseen places.* Of course, saying that wouldn't go over well, or be wise, so he moved his feet in the direction that Lily and Ryan went.

---

SARAFINA TURNED on the cold water. What she wouldn't give to splash her face with it. Then she'd ruin her makeup, of course. But she needed something to cool down the heat swarming every inch of her body. Standing next to Dax for over an hour, him holding her waist as if he were made to fit next to her had been the worst torture she could imagine.

She had expected a quick round of pictures, because Lily truly hated taking pictures as much as her, but Lily's mother had different plans. Posing this way, standing that way. A never-ending parade of shots that would look great to reminisce later in life, but hadn't been that necessary.

The entire time, Sarafina could see Lily chomping at the bit to end the picture taking, but every time her mouth opened to say, "Great, we got them all," her mother would pipe in with another round of pictures in a new spot.

She knew every last picture would look perfect and serene. The hotel, not only elegant in the architecture and style, also had a lovely inside garden. A bundle of trees and flowers guided by a marbled-stone path that looped around a glorious water fountain. Benches were scattered around the path with a fine, articulate oak crafted gazebo ending the long maze. Without venturing into the ballroom yet, she had to say the garden was her favorite part of the hotel.

Entering the ballroom hadn't filtered into her mind. No. She needed some space, a little breather after standing so close to the one man she shouldn't fantasize about. He was off-limits, especially with Lora making her intentions clear.

Despite the pain of standing for nearly an hour next to

such drool-worthy heaven, her face almost frozen in a smile, it had been a glorious time. Dax had whispered constantly into her ear, saying silly nonsense that made her want to laugh with a snort attached to it. He could say the most outrageous things that normally wouldn't sound humorous from anyone else. It had to be the way it left his mouth in such a hot, erotic whisper, his warm breath tickling down her body as each word caressed her.

Because she couldn't help herself, him making every-thing so easy, she whispered back in his ear, countering every silly thing he said. He managed to make a drawn-out hour into something magical.

Hence the immediate retreat. She needed to re-center herself. Falling for him would be wrong. Stupid and entirely wrong.

With that reminder firmly in place, she shut the water off, wiped her hands with a lacy hand towel, and exited the bathroom.

Entering the ballroom, the ambiance of the place centered her back into a balance she could handle. Decora-tions of glittering white lights hung from the ceiling, accom-panied by white lanterns lit up with candles. It gave the room such a magical glow. Centered in the middle of the room, an ice sculpture of hands embracing a heart looked perfect with the setting.

Love.

Pure love surrounded this room.

Lily and Ryan. Her eyes zoomed to them immediately talking to a cluster of people, hands together, bodies molded as one. Just pure love.

And pure jealousy. Why couldn't she find that? All she wanted was someone to love her like Ryan obviously did with Lily. Was that too much to ask for?

"Finally, the most beautiful woman in this place makes her appearance," a sweet, sexy voice said from behind her.

She slowly turned around, her lips wide with happiness. "Does that make you the handsomest man in this place?"

Travis, Lily's older brother, made a stylish bow. "But, of course, madam."

"Shouldn't your sister be the most beautiful woman here?"

He looped his arm around her waist, guiding her to the bar to the left. "Let me buy you a drink. And Lily is quite beautiful, but you're neck and neck with her. What can I say? I can't resist a beautiful woman."

She laughed, playfully slapping his chest. "You are such a heartbreaker. We both know you can't buy me a drink since it's an open bar. How about a dance?"

"A woman after my own heart. I would love to dance with you." He guided her to the dance floor where, just in time, a slow song started to play. Pulling her effortlessly into his arms, he held her gently as the song began. "Where's your lucky man tonight?"

"You know I came here date-free. All men stink. Didn't you know that?"

He laughed with her, his eyes twinkling with delight. "They do, don't they? Men are such assholes. I'm glad you came alone. More time for me to weasel my way into your embrace. And look, you're right where I wanted you from the beginning."

She rested her head onto his chest as she tried to stifle her laughter. Lifting her eyes again, she brushed a soft hand across his cheek. "If only we didn't see each other as brother and sister, what a perfect couple we'd make."

His eyes dipped into sadness for a brief moment before

flickering back to the happy Travis she always saw. What was that sadness?

"If only. Life would be so much easier. Any eyes on a particular someone tonight? It is a wedding. Love is in the air. It's hard not to want to fall for someone."

Sarafina shook her head, not wanting to admit any such thing, her eyes unwittingly landing on Dax, who stood on the other side of the room mingling with guests. Their eyes met briefly, her looking away first, unnerved by what she saw.

"I'm here to enjoy the night and happily go home alone. How about you? What lucky lady will be joining you tonight?"

He glanced around the room, making an exaggerated play, like he was delicately choosing his prey for the night. "Lady to our two o'clock. I like her smile."

She peeked at the woman in question, chuckling as she rolled her eyes. "Or you like the nice set of breasts she has. They're likely to fall out at any moment."

He grinned like the devil, the seduction clear. "That looks nice on her as well. It's her smile that drew me in, though."

"How about the woman to our six? She's beautiful."

Barely sparing a glance, Travis shook his head. "Not happening. She's a nice girl."

"You know her?"

"No. She's somebody from Ryan's side, but she has nice girl written all over her. You don't take a nice girl home from a wedding. You take an easy girl. Less complicated. They know what's going to happen and aren't heartbroken the next day when you have absolutely no intention of calling her."

"You're horrible. You are a heartbreaker," she said, patting his chest with a small chuckle.

"I'm a realist with honesty. I'm simply looking to get laid, unless you want to change your mind about me being a brother figure to you."

His cocky yet sweet grin almost had her melting in her shoes, except, no matter how hard she tried, she could never see him as anything but an older brother. "Sure. Let's find an empty closet now. I'm suddenly horny."

His laughter filled up the room. Bending down, he kissed her cheek, brushing his mouth near her ear. "Damn, Fina, you are a woman I could easily fall in love with. It really is a shame."

"Yeah, that's why all the men keep walking out of my life like a revolving door."

"None of them were good enough. I'm not sure there's a man alive good enough for you. You're too wonderful."

"So, you're saying I'm a nice girl."

"Definitely a nice girl. Any man who takes you home tonight will know that. And you know you'd never do the one-night stand thing. You'd expect a call the next day. That being said, let me know what man has any intention of bringing you home tonight and I'll tell you what's on his mind. I'm not letting any asshole mark you as an easy woman."

"Rest assured, Travis, I won't be going home with anyone tonight."

"Nobody? What about Dax, Ryan's friend? I've seen you two laughing and talking a lot today."

She rolled her eyes, trying to dispel any reaction that said she would love it if he took her home. "We were paired together. Am I supposed to ignore the man? Plus, Lora staked her claim. I would never barge in on that."

"Forget about her. Dad already put a stop to that."

"What do you mean?"

"He told Lora to stay away from Dax. He doesn't know him, and you know how Dad gets. Ryan picking a guy he hasn't seen for almost ten years as a groomsman set Dad off a little. He had someone else in mind, but Ryan told him he already asked Dax. Lily was there, so Dad backed off for once."

"Dax is very nice. I don't understand why he wouldn't like him, or why he'd tell Lora to back off."

Travis cocked an eyebrow. "Seriously, you know Dad when it comes to people he doesn't know. I thought you'd be happy. I saw a little twinkle in your eye when you were talking with Dax. Or was I wrong?"

"It's a wedding, not a business deal. He shouldn't be so concerned about Dax. I saw nothing that would warrant concern." Although, the flash of anger between Ryan and Dax as they walked down the aisle flickered into her mind. "I'm not looking for a man. Dax is very nice, but hardly my type."

"Perhaps you need to change your type."

"Are you suggesting, Travis Chilani, that I make a play for Dax?"

Before answering, he gazed at Dax, then a quick look at his father. "No. I don't know anything about him either. And after all the losers you've dated prior, I think I want to screen any man who may be in the running with you."

"So a full background check on him and then it's a go," she said with a chuckle.

He laughed as well, but his eyes flickered with concern. "Something like that."

"Is everything okay?"

"Of course. Why wouldn't everything be okay?"

"You know you can always tell me anything."

"It's been a crazy day. A crazy week, really." He shrugged, trying to display a smile that didn't reach his eyes. "Dad's been getting a little more aggressive about me joining the family business. I like what I'm doing. I have no interest in stepping into his shoes."

"Then don't. I'm sure he'll understand. You did go to college, and you have been working at the law firm for a few years now. Why would he suddenly make you change course and enter the family business?"

He sighed heavily, twirling her with a dramatic flair, obviously trying to hide the fact the question was a difficult one. She noticed anyway. "That was to let me spread my wings some. It was always temporary. He wants me in the family business, and there's no way I can say no. I'm afraid it's coming a lot sooner than I expected. I guess I have to work on hiding my emotions better if you noticed something was bothering me."

She swiped a tender hand across his cheek. "No, I'm just very tuned in to people's emotions, especially people I truly care about. You're like family to me, Travis. I hate seeing this pain on your face. I know how your father can be, so I know it wouldn't be easy trying to explain how you feel, but it couldn't hurt to try. Perhaps your job could be beneficial to the family business."

Expecting his eyes to light up with happiness at an alternative, she was surprised to see a bit of horror enter. "No, I would prefer to keep my job and the family business separate. It's inevitable, my joining the business. I need to suck it up and move on. There's nothing I can do about it."

He continued to whisk her across the dance floor, the conversation dying as those words twirled around them. As soon as the song ended, he pulled her off the dance floor with the same elegant grace he displayed bringing her onto it.

"Fina, what we talked about…let's keep that between us. It wouldn't do well for my father to hear about my reservations. I can trust you to keep it a secret."

Kissing him lightly on the cheek, she hugged him fiercely. "Your secrets are always safe with me. You know that, Travis."

"You truly would be my perfect match. If I didn't love you so much as a sister, I would pursue you until you gave in to my wily charms."

"It wouldn't take much pursuing. I'd probably fall at your feet with ease."

He laughed, tossing an arm around her waist. "Just my luck. Are you ready for that drink yet?"

"Yes, I think I am. We can talk more about what woman you should set your sights on tonight. I'm not liking the jug-a-lug woman. Her appearance screams easy. Let's find one that's easy, but she shows it more subtly."

"If you insist." He sighed dramatically, yet his face lit up with delight.

"I do insist. Nothing but the best for you."

# 4

Swiping another glass of champagne from the passing tray, Dax took a deep swig before reminding himself he needed to tone down the drinking. He was supposed to be working, not getting shit-faced.

The thought was appealing, though, especially every time he saw Sarafina's beautiful face—and he saw it a lot, considering he purposely made a point to seek her out. Unobtrusively, of course. It wouldn't do well for her to know he was looking at her, or anyone else. Particularly Martin Chilani, or even Travis Chilani.

He didn't have a full dossier on Travis. But there wasn't much to report since, as far as they could tell, he wasn't involved hands-on in the organization. His criminal activity didn't concern Dax at the moment. No. He wanted to know what his relationship to Sarafina was.

Dancing, laughing, even some kissing had been going on between the two, making him want to break something every time his lips connected with her. Sure, it wasn't on the actual mouth. A peck on the cheek here, another peck on the cheek there. But his lips anywhere on her for any reason made Dax want to get his gun and shoot him.

He shouldn't be having this reaction, especially over a woman he just met. Every time his eyes glossed to her, the protective feelings swarmed inside, begging to be released.

The fact was, Travis Chilani couldn't be trusted. His last name assured that he couldn't be trusted, and he wanted him nowhere near Sarafina just for that reason.

But it wasn't that easy. He couldn't waltz up to her and tell her why she should maintain her distance from any member of the Chilani family, Lily included. She would certainly look at him like horns were sticking out of his hair and he was perhaps a little crazy in the head. Questions would be asked, suspicions would rise, and his cover would be blown.

The best thing he could do was wipe her from his memory. Forget she ever existed. She was merely another female who would complain in his ear that he didn't talk enough, or that he worked too much, or he didn't show her enough affection. Just another woman.

His eyes zoomed in on her again as she continued making her rounds around the ballroom, talking, laughing, and enjoying herself with everyone. Most from the Chilani family or connections to the family.

Damn his concern for her. Not only protective-like either. How much knowledge did she have of the family? What if she knew all about their operations? Was she dating Travis, fully aware of what happened behind closed doors? Could he extract all of his intel he needed from her?

Her face lit up with delight as she laughed at what her companion said, a halo of innocence surrounding her.

How could he use her to complete his job? He didn't want to believe she could be involved or have any knowledge about these people. Pretending ignorance would be best. He wasn't sure he'd have the gumption to slap a pair of handcuffs on her.

No. He knew he couldn't. Without much effort, she had carved her way into his heart, ramming a stake in with clear velocity. He barely knew her, but he cared about her. Cared about keeping her out of trouble.

"Why are you over here brooding by yourself?" Ryan asked, taking a sip of his drink as he took a spot next to Dax leaning against the wall.

"Not brooding, observing."

"Definitely brooding. I know brooding when I see it, especially when it comes from you."

Dax's eyes sliced to Ryan, arching a brow with amazement. "When it comes to me, huh? And how would you know?"

"Four years of rooming together in college. I do believe we learned the ins and outs of each other pretty well. I know when you're brooding, and I know when it has to do with a female. Why haven't you been attached to Fina like I thought you'd be?"

"I'm here to work. Plus, she doesn't seem to care that I'm not over by her. What's her relationship with Travis?"

Ryan took another sip before responding. "I don't believe there is one. She's close to the family. That's all."

"Looked to me like there was a lot more than being close to the family."

"Well, if you're not looking for a woman, especially Sarafina, why do you care?"

Dax tore his eyes away from her, not caring where he directed his stare, as long as it wasn't on her. "I don't care."

"What happened to you after college? I tried to call you a few times, but you always ignored me. I would like to agree when you tell people we simply lost touch, but it was more like you just dropped off the face of the earth."

Dax took a deep breath, then downed the rest of his champagne. "Not the place for that kind of conversation."

"After my honeymoon, let's have a beer and talk."

"I thought you were pissed at me for ruining your wedding."

Ryan shrugged, glancing down at the floor. "Well, it hasn't exactly been ruined. Besides a few questions, because people in this family are generally curious, nobody has given you a second glance. It'd be nice to have our friend-ship back. I've missed it over the years."

Rubbing his jaw, Dax wanted to avoid eye contact, but he knew that was the coward's way out. "I missed it, too, man. And I'll continue to miss it. We can't have contact after this. We created a cover that will hopefully hold. If Martin Chilani ever found out I work for the FBI, I would still be a dead man. Maybe even you. I won't risk that. I want you to have a nice, happy life with your new wife. I would never risk putting you in harm's way. It's just the way it has to be."

"I figured you were going to say something like that. That sucks."

Dax barely laughed, finding no amusement in those words. "Tell me about it. Imagine how I felt when my boss told me what was going to happen. I never wanted to do this to you."

Ryan slapped a hand on his shoulder. "I know. I see that now. I was really pissed off at first. I wanted Lily to have the wedding of her dreams. She's been happy so far. Thank you for not ruining anything."

"I never planned to."

"Did you find what you were looking for? Did this whole ruse work?"

Dax shrugged. If he had, he wouldn't tell Ryan. "Night's not over yet."

"When you talked to Mr. Chilani, I guess he didn't spill everything to you."

Dax laughed. "If only it were that easy." He clapped Ryan on the shoulder. "Do you feel a noose yet?"

"I never will. I love her. And when you find the right woman, you won't feel trapped either. You only have to find the right one."

"Yeah, I don't think that's going to happen any time soon." His eyes pinned onto Sarafina like a heat-seeking missile, wondering if maybe he was wrong in his choice of words.

---

She could feel his eyes on her, but every time she chanced a glance, he wasn't staring in her direction. Yet, the moment she turned away, she felt his heated gaze.

Sarafina knew she was torturing herself for no apparent reason. He clearly wasn't interested. No matter all the kind words, silly laughs they shared, he hadn't felt a connection like she obviously had. He had said he wanted a dance with her back at the church. She was still waiting for him to claim that dance.

Lying to her that he couldn't dance wouldn't fly as an excuse either. She saw him on the dance floor several times already, moving to the songs with an ease that spoke volumes. Circling the room like a vulture, he talked to many different people, but his path never brought him near her. She wanted to scream with frustration.

Typical. Just another typical man saying sweet things to turn into a no-good, lying skunk. If he didn't want anything to do with her, he should've never said he wanted to dance with her. Darn that man!

Space. Some air. A breather would be good. Sarafina left the ballroom, intending to use the bathroom, but found herself walking to the gardens instead. Taking in the beauty of the gardens, lit with soft lights from the ceiling to imitate stars, she breathed in a bout of peace.

Why didn't they create this to show the real sky? To see the night sky would make this place even more magical. The lights gave it a surreal look, but it would never compare to the real thing. Perhaps it hadn't been feasible, or maybe it never crossed the architect's mind. Regardless, it would've added to the beautiful ambiance of the room if they had created a sunroof.

Taking her time walking down the path, she wondered if she should make the first move. Maybe Dax was shy, not sure if he should make a move. Or maybe he was trying to recover from Lora retracting her beautiful body from his side. Had he been looking at her with those heated eyes or Lora? Lora said he was looking at her. In the moment, she agreed. When he didn't ignore Lora in the limo and acted interested in her, she changed her opinion. Those heated stares had been meant for Lora.

Why did life have to be so confusing? Men in general.

She started to make her way toward the gazebo when she heard a familiar voice.

She stopped in her tracks, barely making a sound. Panic threatened. *Don't panic.* That would be very bad.

"You know how MC hates when shipments aren't on time. He expects everything to run smoothly. What you're telling me does not reassure me that things will run according to plan. Get your ass in gear and make this shit happen. I want everything on Pier 9 tomorrow at midnight. Not a second late. Have I made myself clear?"

A moment of silence.

"Good. Don't make me take action that you wouldn't like. You know the consequences when shit goes wrong. Do you really want to be on the receiving end of that?"

Another pause.

"I didn't think so. Don't call me again. I'm trying to enjoy myself."

She heard rustling, like he had shoved the phone into his pocket, then footsteps make their way toward her. Oh, darnation. She couldn't let him see her. Dashing into the flowers, she crouched behind a low bush.

Her heart beat like a jackhammer as she waited in hiding, barely covered entirely by the bush, but she must've been hidden well enough when the footsteps never slowed as they passed her. Waiting a few minutes, not wanting to risk being seen, she stayed behind the bush, going over everything she overheard.

Shipment? Consequences? MC? What did it mean? Who in the world was Franklin talking to?

She never did like Lily's cousin Franklin. The man always gave her the worst jitters when he was near. His tone of voice and harsh words didn't help her impression either. That hadn't been a happy phone call, that's for sure. Never trusting him, and hearing a few unsavory things, she didn't think he had been talking about anything legal. She wouldn't be surprised if he was involved in criminal activity, especially considering he had a record for drugs. She didn't know anything beyond that, just a short conversation she had with Lily one time about him getting arrested for having cocaine.

Figuring she hid long enough, she stood up slowly,

peeking back and forth before making her way through the flowers and back onto the path. She made a quick pit stop in the bathroom to make sure she didn't get dirty from the garden and removed a bit of dirt from her shoes. Tempted to leave the party already, she took a deep breath and headed back to the ballroom with a smile on her face.

Barely making it into the room without managing to calm her racing heart, Franklin suddenly appeared at her side.

"May I have this dance, Fina?"

Oh, jeepers, no.

She had no chance to decline when he curled his grimy hand around her waist and pulled her onto the dance floor.

"Where did you run off to? I've been wanting a dance with you all night." His eyes slowly trailed down her face, landing on her breasts with a predatory glare. His hands made a similar trail as they glided down her back to rest on her butt.

Not wanting to make a scene, but also unwilling for him to touch her there, she moved his hands to her back. "Ladies room. I think I had a few too many drinks, and what do they call it...breaking the seal. Unfortunately, I may have done that."

Show no fear. He had no idea she heard his phone conversation. Or did he? Was that why he latched onto her the moment she reentered the ballroom? Did he know she was there and heard everything? Or was he being the annoying leech he always displayed toward her?

He laughed. It sounded more like a cackle to her ears. "Ah, yes, that does tend to happen. Perhaps I can escort you to the bathroom next time to make sure you make it safely. The night is getting late and people are getting more inebriated. I don't trust the look of some of the men."

"That's very kind of you, Franklin, but—"

"Oh my God, I'm having a bride freak-out." Lily grabbed Sarafina's arm, ripping her out of Franklin's arms. "I need to borrow Fina. You understand, Frankie, don't you?"

His expression told her he was pissed by the intrusion, but he nodded. "Of course. We wouldn't want any issues to arise on your day. The night's been going well. I'm not sure why you'd suddenly be having a freak-out."

"Dress malfunction." Lily smiled, then pulled Sarafina away to a dark corner of the room. "Pretend you're messing with the bustle of my dress."

"Thank you. How did you know?" Sarafina asked as she fiddled with Lily's dress, eyeing a button that had actually become loose.

"You've never liked Frankie. The minute I saw him pull you onto the dance floor, I knew I had to save you. Or were you enjoying yourself?"

"Jeepers, no. His grimy hands made a play for my butt the minute he pulled me out there. He has no respect. I feel like I need a shower now."

"Sorry. He's such a loser. How come I haven't seen you dance with Dax yet?"

Sarafina wished she could avoid that answer, not even sure how to answer it. It was a very good question. "I haven't? The night's still young."

Lily stepped away. "My dress is fine now."

"Actually, you had a loose button. I fixed it. Crisis averted."

Lily looped her arm around Sarafina's and started walking. "Thank you. I knew you'd fix my crisis. Now, let's fix yours."

"What crisis? You already fixed that when you saved me

from Franklin." Sarafina had a difficult time keeping up with Lily's quick movements.

"Not that one, silly. This one," she whispered as she stopped in front of Dax, who sat at a table by himself. "Dax, Fina needs to rest for a moment. Her feet are starting to ache from those blasted heels I made her wear. I'm such a bridezilla. Do you mind if she sits with you?"

He looked like he'd seen a ghost when she said that, but nodded with a tentative smile. "Of course."

"What are you doing?" Sarafina whispered into her ear.

"Fixing your crisis. There was a spark between you two. I saw it. Now quit avoiding it. Talk to the man." Lily smiled, then pulled out a chair for Sarafina and walked away.

"Sorry about that. If you want me to sit somewhere else, I can."

Dax smiled tenderly at her this time, his eyes sparkling with desire. At least, she interpreted it that way. Hoped. Wished upon a star. Anything to make that look in his eyes real and honest.

"I'd like the company. As funny as it may sound, my feet ache a little as well. New shoes."

"Are you enjoying yourself? I know you don't really know anyone but Ryan."

"I am. I've met a lot of people. It's been nice getting to know everyone. Ryan's a lucky man. Lily seems very special."

"She is. They're a beautiful couple. And, as much as I've enjoyed this evening, I think I'm almost ready to go home."

Why did she say that?

Her face flamed with heat. Jeepers, he would totally interpret that in the wrong way. What an idiot.

"I know what you mean. Another hour or two left. We can manage that, huh?"

Or maybe he hadn't. So much for thinking she saw a spark of desire. "Yeah, we can."

Then he looked at her, his eyes saying something, yet she wasn't exactly sure what. Did she really want to know what they were saying?

"I'm sorry about Lora."

His eyebrows rose. "Sorry? I'm not sure what you mean."

"You two seemed to hit it off in the limo, then she sort of ditched you. She's a beautiful woman."

"She is." Resting his elbow on the table, he leaned closer. "She's not as beautiful as you. I'm not sorry she walked away. Confused, maybe, because she was giving me clear signals, but definitely not sorry."

"I can clear up that confusion for you."

He leaned back in his chair. "How's that?"

"You don't know much about the Chilani's, do you?"

"I only met them today."

For some reason, she felt like he was avoiding her question by not answering it clearly. "Mr. C is the head of the family. Then comes Mrs. C, and so on and so forth."

"Mr. C? Martin Chilani, you mean."

She nodded.

"I imagine he is. He is the father. Normally, they are the head of the family."

"Yeah, but I mean it in a different sense. Everyone, including extended family, listen to him. If he says something, you listen."

He nodded, understanding her better. "Does that include you? Do you listen to him as well?"

"Of course. He's like my second father. If Lily got into trouble, I was normally tagging along getting a firm talk as well from him. I don't know how many times we snuck out of her house, just to get caught in the act. He was pretty understanding, except that one time."

Leaning forward again, almost reaching his hand toward hers that rested on the table, he asked, "What happened that 'one time?'"

"We snuck out, like usual, to go to a party. Of course, we weren't old enough to drink yet, but that never stopped us. Mr. C was pretty laid back about our nightly adventures, but that time he flew through the roof when we got back."

"Because you were out drinking?"

"No. He berated us for that, but it was for losing our detail. He hated that. I had never seen him so angry before. It scared me."

His brows dipped into confusion, concern marring his features. "Detail? Do you mean bodyguards?"

Sarafina glanced around and bit her lip. Why did she bring this up? Should she be talking to him about this? She probably shouldn't, but he made it easy to forget that she barely knew him.

"Yes, that's what I mean. Mr. C does a lot of international business. What that entails, I have no clue, but he always makes sure the safety of his children is his main concern. He didn't mind us sneaking out, as long as we had our detail following us. So, really, we weren't sneaking out, but he was giving us a chance to act like normal teenagers. He was so upset that night because we managed to slip our detail. Lily and I had the greatest laugh that we actually managed to do it."

"I know you said you don't really know what his business entails, but why would he think bodyguards are necessary?"

"I know he deals with a lot of money. You can tell from this wedding that he has a lot. Over the years, there's been a few threats to the family. I don't know the details of that either, just rumors. I remember Lily telling me about a time when someone tried to snatch her when she was little. I didn't know her at the time, but she remembered it being the worst feeling in the world. Bodyguards are a part of her life. I've even gotten used to them. It's almost like they don't exist, they blend in so well. And they have come in handy. I was with her one time when this creep came out of nowhere, trying to force her into a car. If not for those bodyguards, she would've been taken right before my eyes. I definitely understand why he was so upset at us that night. Anything could've happened."

"And that doesn't make you wonder why people would want to snatch Lily, or threaten the family?"

"Money. They're rich. Isn't that what happens when you're rich? People want what you have. That's all Lily is to them. A bargaining chip." She saw his eyes roam around the room. "Yes, Mr. C has bodyguards here tonight."

"I didn't notice."

"Why would you? You don't know the Chilani family as well as I do."

She scooted her chair closer to him, leaning into him, seeking his heat. Her eyes met his as they shared a look of desire. Or at least, she hoped that's what she saw. Before she could find out, she pointed a small finger to their left. "He's a bodyguard. They all blend in well."

He tore his eyes away from her to look where she pointed to a man in a black suit holding a glass of champagne talking to a group of people. Nothing too obvious going on, except for the frequent roll of the man's eyes as he surveyed the room discreetly.

"I would've never guessed. Who else is one? Just curious."

Placing an arm on the table, almost like he was wrapping a protective arm around her, she started to point out, unobtrusively, each person that she knew was a bodyguard. She hadn't realized it until she finished, the tiny sensations of ecstasy coursing through her skin were from the subtle brushes of his fingers against her back.

"So, this entire conversation started because you were sorry that Lora lost interest in me. Why is that again?" he asked, his mouth delicately close to her ear.

"Because Mr. C told her to back off. He doesn't know you, therefore, doesn't trust you. Lora never disobeys her father. Like I said, he's the head of the family. Travis told me this. And I proceeded to tell Travis that you're very nice and there was no reason not to trust you."

"You talked to Travis about me?"

"He was curious about you, wondering what I thought. You're a bit of a mystery to the family. They don't particularly like mysteries. I told him there was nothing to worry about when it came to you. Was I wrong?"

# 5

SUCH A LOADED QUESTION. *Was I wrong?*

Hell yeah, wanted to spill from his lips. Trusting him would be the worst thing she could do. Yet, here she sat, trusting him as if she had known him forever. If she ever found out the real reason he was here, she'd hate him.

Pointing out bodyguards, helping him figure out which were Martin Chilani's men without much effort. He had pegged a few himself, but she helped point out the rest. She had no clue how useful that information was. He felt like the biggest asshole using her.

"You have nothing to worry about."

There. Question answered without really answering. She truly had nothing to worry about. He would never harm her or slap a pair of handcuffs on her. He was starting to think she might know more than he realized. Was she really that clueless when it came to what Martin Chilani actually did?

International business. That's what she thought he did. Did she not know what that business entailed? Gunrunning, drugs, murder.

Dax hoped she was clueless.

"So are you sad?"

He lost where this conversation went. What was he supposed to be sad about? Lora?

"She's not my type. She was coming on strong and I didn't want to hurt her feelings, so I played along. I'm not sad."

"That was nice of you. She does come on strong." She glanced down at her lap like she wanted to say more but was afraid to say it.

"You and Travis seem close. You looked like you were enjoying yourself out on the dance floor with him."

What the hell was wrong with him? Why would he let her know he had been watching her? But damn it, he wanted to know what was going on between them.

"Oh, we are close." Blushing fiercely, her eyes got round with shock. "Like brother and sister, I mean. Close like that. He's like my annoying older brother I never had. I have a younger brother. He annoys me at times, too."

"That's good."

"Why's that?"

She looked at him with an unreadable expression. His arm was locked around her, his fingers brushing her back, completely unable to stop even if he wanted to. She hadn't objected, so he felt no need to stop. Inches away from her mouth, he could close the distance to answer another loaded question. That would answer it plenty. It would also be wrong. He had one objective tonight: to learn the location of the load of weapons coming in. So far, he was failing miserably.

And, it seemed, so was his self-control. "Maybe I was a bit jealous. I still haven't gotten my dance I reserved earlier today."

"You didn't ask me for a dance yet. I've been waiting."

"Have you? You've been busy dancing the night away. Hell, I noticed you didn't even finish the last dance when Lily yanked you away. Perhaps you want to finish that one first."

There was no mistaking the shiver that rushed through her body.

"What did I say? What's the matter?" Did his jealousy come out that obvious?

"Dancing with Franklin is the furthest thing from my mind. I was happy when Lily saved me from him. Trust me. I'd much rather dance with you."

His hand tightened on her back as he gently laid a hand on her leg. "What aren't you saying? Why does he scare you? And don't try to lie to me. I can see that he scares you."

"Franklin has always been the creepy cousin. He looks at me like a piece of meat, and it unnerves me every time. I've never liked him. And he's a criminal."

That perked Dax up. *Don't get excited.* But damn if he couldn't help it. Still earning the title of an asshole. He needed to coax more out of her.

"Criminal? What do you mean?"

"Oh, I know he's been arrested for drugs before. Maybe not that serious, but I don't trust him." She looked away, shaking her head with disgust. "Jeepers, I wouldn't be surprised if what I heard him say had to do with drugs. He's not a good person."

Holy shit. Were the answers he needed right in front of him? He didn't want Sarafina to be the answer to his prayers. He wanted her to be clueless, innocent, and so far away from any danger.

"When did you hear him say something? What was it?"

She waved her hand like she was dismissing everything

she just said. "It was probably nothing. He scares me. I heard him in the gardens earlier talking to someone and it all sounded weird. Like I said, he always creeps me out. I'm probably making him sound bad when he truly isn't."

*Don't count on that.*

"Well, I hope it had nothing to do with drugs here tonight. I'd hate for Ryan and Lily's night to be ruined." *You're such an asshole, Dax. Why are you playing her like this?*

"Oh, no, I know it's not tonight. I would never let that happen. I wouldn't want Lily's night to be ruined for anything. I probably wouldn't let her know, but maybe would've said something to Mr. C. I could still say something to him. I don't know why I said anything."

"I don't mind. Sometimes, telling someone helps you determine whether it's important or not. I'm all ears to be a sounding board, if you think you should tell Mr. Chilani." *Please, Sarafina, tell me, not that man. You could be seriously hurt.*

She bit her lip again, the indecision clear. He loosened his hand on her back and started to rub softly like before.

"He sounded angry on the phone. He told the person, whoever he was talking to, that MC doesn't like delays and to have the shipment tomorrow night at midnight without delay. Not a second later." Her body clouded with trembles.

Hot damn. He couldn't believe his ears. The information he needed simply tossed out of her mouth like she had no clue, which he clearly believed. She had absolutely no clue that what she overheard she really shouldn't have. And MC? Couldn't she see the connection? That clearly stood for Martin Chilani.

He had the time. Midnight tomorrow. Now he needed a location.

"Hmm, sounds a little dubious. What does Franklin do as a job? Maybe he was just talking about work. Did he mention anything else?" Heart pounding like mad, he hoped against all hope she couldn't tell how nervous he was to hear her answer.

"That's a good point." She laughed like she was an idiot. "He works near the docks, doing what, I have no clue. He goes from job to job a lot, and honestly, I try to forget that man even exists. He said something about Pier 9. You're right. It's probably related to his job and he doesn't want to get into any trouble with his boss. Forget I said anything."

Dax laughed with her to ease the unspoken tension. "That's probably all it was. I have no problem forgetting about him. What I don't want to forget is dancing with you." He stood up, holding his hand out. "Will you dance with me?"

Shyly, she placed her hand into his. "I thought you'd never ask."

Wrapping her perfectly into his arms, they moved to the slow beat like she was born to fit into his arms. "This is the best dance of the night."

Without turning away, her face shaded to a faint red as she said, "Is this you being nice, playing along to make me feel good?"

"You mean, like I did with Lora?"

"Yes," she whispered breathlessly, almost as if she were afraid to voice it.

The best answer would be to say yes. Lie to her. Don't encourage anything. But he already hated all the lies between them. No more worries about his job anymore. To his great surprise, he retrieved the information he had been seeking. How that happened, he wasn't too happy about. He sure in the hell wouldn't be letting his boss know it came from Sarafina. He'd deal with the potential fallout later if it came to it. There was no way in hell he would drag her anywhere near this mess.

Because he was here for a job, he should say yes. Tear whatever was happening between them off like a band-aid. Fast and clean. He shouldn't even be entertaining anything with her.

"No. This isn't me being nice. Ignoring you for the entire evening was me being nice."

"That doesn't sound very nice to me."

Bending his head, his mouth brushed her ear as he took a small nibble. "Giving in to my feelings for you would lead to nothing good. Trust me, Sarafina. Keeping my distance was me being nice. Giving in to what I crave is just being selfish." He sucked on her earlobe, then placed a tender kiss on her neck before looking into her eyes. He was such a jerk. Why did he continue to torture them both?

"I've wanted you since I met you. I'm dying to take you away from this place and lock you in a room with just the two of us. I'm dying to explore what's underneath this beautiful dress. But I can't do any of that. You deserve more than what I can give."

There. A little honesty for once. And it killed him to utter each word.

———

SHE WAS A NICE GIRL. Wasn't that what Travis said? Any man who wanted to take her home would know that. Clearly, Dax knew that but refused to indulge in sweet pleasure with her knowing he only wanted a one-night stand.

Could she do a one-night stand? Was she that type of girl?

No. She wasn't.

But for Dax, the thought sounded appealing. She wanted him. How could she deny them the pleasure? Maybe he would reconsider. Maybe it could turn into more than a one-night stand.

Of course, wasn't that what all women thought?

No. Only nice girls thought that. The other women knew the terms when it came to a one-night stand. But maybe he would see how good they could be together if she let him take her home.

Was she really contemplating this? What happened to keeping her distance? He was the wrong man for her. Completely wrong. Until he nibbled on her ear and pressed his warm lips to her skin, concluding he was perfect for her. She couldn't stop the inferno roaring inside her body, or function to think normally.

"Sarafina, I feel like I lost you. What are you thinking?"

She tore her gaze away from his chest to look him straight in the eyes. "I was thinking how wonderful your lips would feel on other parts of my body."

Did she just say that? She didn't say things like that.

"God, you're torturing me." He pulled her closer, letting her feel how strongly he wanted her. "Trust me. You'd hate me the next day."

"Not if we're clear what this is."

"And what is this? What do you think this is between us?"

"A strong sexual attraction, probably from the start. What's so wrong with giving in to that attraction?"

His feet moved with quick precision, yet gracefully, as he

steered them to some privacy. Off the dance floor, away from the crowd, he grabbed her cheeks gently in his hands. "Listen to me. I can't give you more than a night. That's all this would be. One night between us. You're not that kind of woman. I won't treat you like that kind of woman."

"Even if it's what I want? I'm always picking out the wrong man, thinking they are sweet, kind, generous, when they turn out to be nothing close to that. I keep telling myself you are wrong for me and to keep my distance. Well, maybe that's what's been wrong all along. I'm pushing the wrong men away. I'll take one night with you. I want to be that kind of woman tonight."

"Listen to your instincts. I am wrong for you. I won't turn you into that. Don't ask me to."

Leaning into him, she ran her hands down his chest. "Because if I ask, you'll give me what I want."

He trembled under her touch, his eyes glistening into maddening desire. "You make it impossible to resist you. Please, Sarafina, I don't want you to hate me. You will. Trust me."

"I'm a big girl, Dax. I can take care of myself. I can take a hint. I'm sorry."

Before she embarrassed herself further by flinging herself into the arms of a man who didn't want her as much as his body said he did, she turned around. Getting one foot in front of her, a strong hand twirled her back around. She slammed into his chest as his mouth came crashing down.

She barely opened her mouth to let him explore when he pulled away, breathing heavily. "Damn it. I don't want to want you. But I can't help myself. Please, whatever happens in the future, know that what's about to happen tonight is because I care for you. I'm risking it all to have this one night. Just one. There can never be more."

Still feeling the taste of him on her lips, she almost had a hard time focusing on his words. "You're confusing me. Are you married? Do you have a girlfriend or something? What are you risking?"

"There's no one in my life. I swear. You either trust me enough to take what I'm offering, or I'll let you walk away for good this time."

The smart thing would be to walk away. His evasiveness, his cryptic words, worried her. Funny thing, she was never very smart when it came to men.

"I think I'm finally ready to go home. I've had enough of this wedding. How about you, Dax? Will you escort me home?"

His hesitation made her worry he changed his mind, but then he spoke. "It'd be my pleasure to make sure you made it home safely."

Pleasure. Yes, there would be plenty of that when they reached her house.

"I have to say good-bye to Lily."

"You do that. I'll meet you outside." He kissed her lightly on the lips and walked away.

Why wouldn't he say good-bye with her? Perhaps he didn't want to be seen leaving together. That would tell everyone what was about to happen tonight. He had the right idea.

Scanning the room for Lily, she saw her with Ryan and Travis. As soon as Lily saw her approach, she stepped away from them.

"Where's Dax? Are you seriously not giving that man a chance?"

"What would you say if I was letting him take me home tonight?"

Lily's face lit up with happiness, until Sarafina gave her a look that said to stay quiet. "What aren't you saying out loud?"

"I'm pretty sure this will be a one-time thing. I don't want you to get your hopes up like this will be a new relationship or anything."

"Ryan has better friends than that. Dax would never treat you like a one-night stand."

"Well, maybe I'm treating him like one. Did you ever think about that? It's been a while, and he's available. I feel like stepping out of my comfort zone for once."

Lily rolled her eyes in disbelief. "I would never believe that in a million years. Clearly, there's something you don't want to say, but that's okay. I'll find out later when you're ready to talk. And based on the looks from Dax, he'd never treat you like that. I know Ryan will be happy."

Sarafina grabbed her arm with panic. "Don't you dare tell Ryan I'm going home with Dax. Please, keep this to yourself. You're right. We'll talk later."

"Fine. Have a great night." Lily hugged her tightly.

"You, too. Have a wonderful honeymoon. We'll talk when you get back."

Sarafina let her go, waved to Ryan and Travis, and started to make her way out of the ballroom. Almost reaching the exit, a hand grabbed her from behind.

"Saying good-bye with only a wave," Travis said as he turned her around to face him.

"How silly of me. Good-bye, Travis." She reached up to kiss him lightly on the cheek and gave him a hug. "Is that better?"

He smiled delightfully. "Much better. Why are you leaving so early?"

"The party's almost over. I'm tired."

"Then I'll leave with you and make sure you get home okay."

Panic lit up in her eyes as she waved her hand. "I'm fine. What happened to the lovely brunette we picked out for you? You're supposed to escort her home."

"I changed my mind. I'm not into an easy lay tonight. I'd rather make sure you get home and then crash in my own bed. Why do I get the impression you have someone else taking you home?"

"What makes you think that?"

"I can always tell when you're being evasive. Care to share who the lucky man is?"

"Not really, no."

He gave her a look that said he wasn't happy with her. "We talked about this. I screen any man who wants to take you home."

"And I changed my mind. I appreciate you acting like the older brother here, but I'm a big girl. I can take care of myself. Sharing with my honorary brother about the man I'm taking home wouldn't be a fair conversation, since I don't even talk like this with my real brother. Understand?"

"No, Fina, I don't understand. I'm not okay with this."

She gently laid a hand on his cheek. "You don't have a say in the matter. I'm sorry if that bothers you, Travis."

"I'm not letting you leave here, until I know who it is. Don't test me, Sarafina."

The way her full name left his lips made her sad in a way she never felt with him before. She could clearly see how upsetting this was, unsure of why it truly bothered him.

"What are you going to do, Travis? Tell me."

Anger emerged on his face. Perhaps she was foolish to test him. He *was* the son of Martin Chilani, a man who always got his way. What made Travis any different?

Her hand dropped from his cheek when he took a step away from her. "I don't think you'd like what I would do, so I'll just say good night. You're right. You can take care of yourself. Don't think this means I forgive you."

"Forgive me? Now you're mad at me."

"I feel many things right now, but I'm not sure anger is one of them. I saw you finally had a dance with Dax."

He knew. She could tell in that one sentence that he knew who was taking her home. And he didn't like it for some reason. "I did. Would you like to get lunch later this week?"

His features dipped down into sadness, but then he nodded. "I'd like that. I'll call you. Can the same thing be said about the man taking you home?"

"Good night, Travis." She kissed him again on the cheek, despite him flinching a little, and left him standing there with the sorrow etched in his features.

Slowly walking to the front of the hotel, she wondered if she was making a colossal mistake. Seeing Dax standing outside on the sidewalk, waiting next to a cab with the door open, his eyes drowning with desire as she walked toward him, she knew. This was no mistake.

"You didn't say good-bye to anyone," she said lightly as she slid into the cab. He followed right behind her.

"I nodded a good-bye at Ryan. That's the only person I needed to say good-bye to. And since I'm taking you home, there wasn't a need to say good-bye to you."

At least, not yet, were the unspoken words she heard. No sense worrying about it. She gently rested her head on his shoulder, sighing with contentment at how right it felt.

"Where are we going? The cab driver needs to know," he whispered softly with a chuckle.

"You have me all forgetful and flustered." She laughed

nervously, then proceeded to rattle off her address to the cab driver.

Twenty minutes later, they made it to her brickstone house nestled nicely on a quiet street at the end of the row of homes. Dax paid the cabbie without hesitation and guided her to the front door with one hand on her back. Surprised the nerves weren't visible, she unlocked the door quickly and stepped inside, flipping on the light.

"Welcome to my humble home. I'm pretty proud of it."

"It's definitely on a nice street. I didn't ask you once tonight what you do. I feel like we're skipping a lot of things and jumping right into something that should be taken slowly."

She flipped the lock, then turned toward him and gazed strongly into his eyes. "Do you want to talk about what I do? Are you changing your mind about giving me more than one night? If you are, I'd be more than happy to talk as long as you want. But if you're not, I prefer to skip a lot of things, as you put it."

Darn, talk about being bold. Where did she learn to talk like this? Or did she just have the brazenness when it came to Dax?

"Screw the talking then. I don't plan to waste a minute of this night talking, unless it's to tell you to get naked." He scooped her into his arms. "Where's the bedroom?"

"Up the stairs, last door to the left. My stairs are very creaky. Sometimes, it makes me think ghosts are living with me."

Taking his time as he climbed the stairs, he chuckled. "Now we're switching the conversation to ghost stories. Is that what you decided you want?"

"No, but let me know if you hear them late at night like I do. Scares the bejesus out of me sometimes."

He paused when he got to the top, eyeing her critically. "Do you check the house out when you hear the noises?"

"I do. I can't help myself. I never find anyone. Like I said, it's ghosts. Creepy, right?"

"Yeah, creepy. I've never seen a ghost before. Don't really want to start tonight. The only thing I want to see is you naked. Right now."

She had been slyly trying to tell him to spend the entire night. Protecting her from ghosts, as lame as it sounded, had been her only good excuse. She honestly could hear moans and creaks throughout the night that did have her quivering with fear at times. That hadn't been a total fib. But his simple statement of *don't really want to start tonight* made her assume he had no intentions of staying until morning. Just long enough to get his fill and leave, apparently. She would take what he was willing to give. How pathetic.

He shoved her bedroom door closed with a kick of his shoe and set her down near the bed. "Are you sure about this, Sarafina? I don't want to hurt you."

"If we go in with our eyes wide open, how can anyone get hurt?"

She had the sinking feeling that as much as she hoped to change his mind, a one-night stand was all she would be getting. One night. No possible way to walk away from this without getting hurt. Having the knowledge that he truly didn't want to hurt her made it not hurt as bad. But there was absolutely no way she could turn him away now. She needed this. Wanted it with every breath in her body. He was worth the hurt.

"I'm going to hell for sure," he whispered right before his lips claimed hers.

She had no chance to ask what that meant. Clearly, he worried about hurting her more than she imagined.

Nothing to worry about now. His hands on her back, slipping the zipper down was all she wanted to worry about.

Her dress slid down with ease, leaving her in nothing but a white, lacy strapless bra, a white lacy thong, and her silver high heels.

He stepped back to let her step out of the dress. His eyes dropped down in surprise, gliding down her body in sensual madness.

"This is what you had on underneath this dress. A thong? You are so lucky I didn't know this at the reception hall."

She started to undo the buttons on his shirt when he made no move to come back into her arms. "Oh yeah. Why's that?"

He tossed his jacket to the floor, his shirt joining shortly after. Grabbing her tightly into his embrace, he lifted her around his waist and brought her to the nearest wall. "All I would've had to do is find an empty room, slide this little piece of fabric to the side and bury myself deep inside you. Nothing to it when you're wearing a damn thong."

"Is that what you're planning on doing now? Having me against this wall as I wear my little thong and high heels?"

His hands cupped her butt, rubbing them gently over her silky skin. Oh, how she wanted them to make their way to her front.

"Hell, no. We have a bed here. I plan on using it. I just wanted you to feel how I would've taken you there if I had known."

He walked over to the bed, laying her down gently. One by one, he slipped her shoes off, tossing them to the floor behind him. Divulging himself of the rest of his clothes, he stood for a moment and let her drink in the sight of him.

Muscled from head to toe, a small trail of chest hair led

down to the ultimate prize. He stood thick and proud, like he couldn't wait to be inside her.

"Do you like what you see, Sarafina?" he asked with a lustful smirk.

She curled her arms behind her head and crossed her feet. "Yes. I could lay here all night and stare at you."

"Tough. I'm not sure how much longer I'll last if I don't have you now." He reached down into his pants pocket, took out his wallet and a condom hidden inside a pocket.

Crawling onto the bed, he straddled her body, sliding his hands behind her back, unhooking her bra with ease. Tossing the garment behind him, he bent down and took a nipple into his mouth with feverish delight.

"You taste so good," he murmured as he swirled his tongue around the hard tip, sucking intensely before moving to her other breast.

Not wanting to regret a moment of this night, she brushed her hands down his back, cupping his butt before running her hands back up. He felt smooth to the touch, the muscles tensing everywhere her hands roamed. She clenched a fistful of hair the minute his hot mouth started to taste the most intimate part of her body. Because she was so ramped up from wanting him, it didn't take long for her to cry out with bliss.

She felt a snap at her waist as he broke her thong off, unaware that he hadn't even taken it off yet. His mouth had captured her undivided attention. Hearing a crinkle or two beside her, still enjoying her moment of bliss, she perked up again when the tip of him started to slowly enter her.

"You feel so damn good, Sarafina. Tell me you have more condoms. I only have one. And once with you will not be enough tonight," he whispered into her ear, nibbling as he did, taking his sweet time to enter her inch by inch.

"I think I have some in the bathroom. I hope so. I'm on the pill. We're safe."

She never in her life said such words. Safe. Since when would having sex without a condom and relying on the pill be safe? Only when it involved Dax, apparently.

"Safe. You're safe in my arms, like I'm safe in yours, right?"

She nodded, too afraid to say anything, her attention more on the way his body moved in and out of her. No more words. Letting the magic build between them seemed like a much better plan.

He moved with a slow caress, taking his time to savor each thrust, each moan that filled the air. She couldn't keep her hands still, the thought that she had to memorize each curve, each muscle on his body, centered deep in her mind. Forgetting a moment of this wasn't acceptable. She needed to sear every part of him into her mind so she could take those memories out later and relive it like it was happening again.

Every time he thrust into her with such tender care, she wondered how she could have ever thought this wouldn't hurt. Crying to sleep would bring her no joy. Clinging to hope would be fruitless. Praying that he changed his mind, a waste of energy. He was giving her everything, knowing this would be their only night together.

What a fool to think otherwise. So darn foolish.

Clutching him tighter as the movements became faster, he locked his lips to hers as the beauty surrounding them became more powerful. Without warning, she let loose everything she had, pouring all of her emotions into the kiss, and let the orgasm of a lifetime take her away.

He came with her on the journey, tensing for a moment,

then limply fell onto her body as their heavy breathing filled the room.

A soft kiss touched her neck as his warm breath trailed down her body. No words were necessary. That kiss said it all. He felt what she felt. Pure magic. True connection. Something so powerful, words could never describe it.

And it would only last for one night.

# 6

DAX LOOKED at the beautiful woman he couldn't get enough of one last time. Slipping his arm from her warm, delicate body had been one of the most torturous things he'd ever done. His eyes couldn't be ripped away as he dressed, watching every slow breath that left her body.

So sweet.

So innocent.

So not his to claim. Yet, that's what he did tonight. Claimed her in a way he had never claimed a woman before. Four separate times he took her to heights she'd probably never experienced before. Maybe she had. But if her responses were any indication to go by, he didn't think so. He showed her what could be the most powerful passion to ever exist between a man and a woman. He also showed her how one rips another person's heart out without thought or compunction.

That's how he felt. His heart was being ripped from his chest and thrown helplessly to the ground with pounding feet destroying every last part of it. How could he have ever thought this one night would be enough?

One night would never be enough. But that's all he'd been given.

Tempted to lean over and give her one more kiss, he walked away instead, afraid the slightest movement would wake her. This was hard enough as it was. Facing her awake would be worse. Spilling his guts about everything sat on the tip of his tongue, and that was the last thing he could do. He would never put her life in danger, and that's exactly what would happen if he told her who he was and what he was trying to do.

He trusted her, but only to a certain extent. She was best friends with Lily Chilani, daughter of Martin Chilani, one of the most notorious mobsters out there. He wasn't sure she would be able to keep this kind of secret from her best friend. It wasn't fair that he had to put that sort of pressure on his own friend's shoulders. Ryan could handle himself.

But Sarafina. His sweet Sarafina. He wouldn't risk that kind of emotion on her.

He quietly let himself out, flipping the bottom lock behind him. The stairs had creaked mercifully like she told him. Standing a few minutes by the front door had been another form of torture. Had she heard him trying to sneak away? The answer, apparently, had been no. Because after standing like an idiot that seemed to go on for ages, no trailing footsteps emerged.

It was for the best. A clean break. No ties. No heavy emotions. Cutting the rope with one quick slice.

Dax hailed a cab, getting out a few blocks later to a subway station. Taking a few different lines before hailing another cab, he made it to his own place over an hour later. Perhaps he was being too careful, but sometimes a man could never be careful enough. In case anyone—one of

Chilani's men—had been outside her home, he didn't want them to follow him home.

Taking a quick shower, washing away all the delicious evidence from the night, he finally sat down at his kitchen counter with a hot, steaming cup of coffee.

Before he could change his mind, he pulled his phone out, hitting the last number he wanted to call.

"Everything set for tonight, Sloan?"

"Yep. You turned your phone off last night after you sent me the text about the location. Not a smart thing to do. What happened?" Sloan, his supervisor, asked with concern.

"Nothing. I needed some time to myself. It wasn't easy betraying my friend like that."

He heard a heavy sigh on the other end, hating himself for making his boss the bad guy. What they did, while difficult, had been the right thing to do.

"Can we trust this information? How did you get it? I need details."

The worst part he had wanted to avoid, to pretend it wouldn't be asked at all, to test his feelings for a woman he shouldn't feel a thing for.

"I overheard a phone conversation. I could only hear Franklin Chilani speaking, but that's the gist of what he said. No idea who he was talking to."

Done.

Lie complete.

Sarafina would never be involved in any way. What difference did it make if he heard the conversation or if she did? Not much. Besides the part where she wasn't involved in any way. That's all he wanted. She needed to stay safe.

"Well, I'd say that's pretty good information then. He is one of Martin Chilani's right-hand men. You can come in, but I don't want you anywhere near that pier tonight or the precinct. We'll call the NYPD for backup."

"Are they all clean? Can we trust them?"

"I have people I can trust there, and that's who I'll call. Martin Chilani doesn't have everyone in his pocket. The most important thing is for you to stay out of the picture. I don't want your cover blown now. This is the critical part."

"You don't have to remind me, boss. I don't want to see Ryan get hurt either. Maybe it's been a long time since I've seen him, but he's still my friend."

"I know. Did everything else go okay last night? Any problems pop up?"

*Besides the part where I met the most amazing woman and can't keep her? Nope, no problems.* "The night went well." He took a sip of coffee to gain some of his equilibrium back. "I even talked to Martin Chilani. He definitely looked me up, trying to test me. He said we would talk some more, but he never came up to me. I didn't want to make anything obvious by pursuing him."

"Good choice. Come in later and write it up, then take the day off. We'll talk more after we have, hopefully, Martin Chilani himself in custody. Did you get the impression he would be there? Our intel said so."

"Based on the conversation, no, I'm not sure." Probably would've been able to give a more solid answer if he actually heard the conversation, but the lie was already out there. No going back now.

Dax hung up with Sloan and roamed around his empty house. Damn it if Sarafina wouldn't look good here. She would fit in perfectly. He lived on the Jersey side, putting up with commuting rather than dealing with the hustle and bustle that he was surrounded by when he worked. His house sat in a small community still being developed, but would still have plenty of space after everything was completed. Would she like it? Would she fall in love with the airiness, the space, the homey feeling like he had right away?

Well, those questions didn't matter. He would never see her again. Just as it should be.

The day went slow. It made Dax want to crawl out of his skin. Going back into the city to write his report, then heading back home had been difficult. The entire time he ached to turn his vehicle toward Sarafina's place rather than his own. Once at home, he had nothing but his tortured mind and memories to get him through the night.

Shortly after midnight, he got a call, the information surprising as hell. Franklin Chilani was in custody for weapons charges, smuggling, and a whole other slew of crimes—petty ones that he would probably skate on. Not the weapon charges. They would make it stick, even if he had to stand over the shoulder of the prosecution the entire time. Make sure they dotted every I and crossed every T.

None of that surprised him.

What shocked him was the arrest of Travis Chilani. What the hell had he been doing there? Nowhere in their reports did it indicate that Travis Chilani had joined the business. Guess dear old dad decided it was time to show his son the ropes.

This news was too good to be true, and wanting to see the man who had made him insanely jealous behind bars, Dax left his place and made his way back into the city once again. When his boss found out, he'd be pissed for sure. But Dax couldn't stay away.

He would stay in the shadows away from prying eyes, but to see Travis in cuffs would make his night. Eyeing the way he held Sarafina, the way he kissed her on the cheek, wrapping his arms around her as if he had a right to, sent him right off the edge. He would enjoy seeing his discomfort sitting behind bars.

They didn't manage to get Martin Chilani, but they were one step closer. His son would do very well as a replacement.

———

SARAFINA BRUSHED another tired hand over her eyes as she tried to wipe the sleep away. Getting no sleep the night before because of a handsome man keeping her awake had deprived her of much-needed sleep. Waking up to an empty bed, alone, had crushed her more than she cared to admit.

She knew it would hurt, the pain like a knife wound to the chest. She just hadn't realized it would hurt so bad that simple functions like eating would become difficult. Moping around the house, barely coherent, had been how her day played out.

Every time she turned, Dax's face pricked her mind. They hadn't explored her home, never leaving her bedroom for anything, but he was still imprinted everywhere. She couldn't walk into any room without thinking about him.

Pathetic.

That's how she felt—again—towards a man. Why did she do this to herself? Last night had been a night to remember. That's it. A distant memory that would pierce her heart until the day she died. He'd been that good, that sweet, that attentive. No man would ever replace him.

And darn it, he had topped off her entire checklist with ease. In one night. Why did he have to seem so perfect?

Going to bed tonight had been futile, to say the least, but she laid down in bed anyway. Tossing and turning, imagining the perfect man she shouldn't, not much sleep came over her.

When her phone rang around four in the morning, she welcomed the distraction. Seeing it was Lily calling had put her in a sudden panic. She should be enjoying her honeymoon on some exotic island, not calling her in the middle of the night.

After hanging up the call, her world turned upside down. She had no idea how she dressed, called a cab, and made it to the police precinct thirty minutes later.

Travis had been arrested.

Never in his life had he gotten in trouble. Sure, she saw the news articles and heard the whispers around Lily's family when Mr. C was arrested a few times. But lies, that's all they were. Mr. C was a good man. She couldn't understand why the police harassed him as they did. Murder, extortion, bribery. A few things she remembered reading about. To think he had anything to do with such things shocked her. Trying to talk to Lily about it hadn't gone well. Ignoring it seemed like the best solution. She couldn't picture Mr. C being the kind of man people tried to make him sound like.

He could be hard, cruel even, at times. But she refused to believe him to be that monstrous.

And Travis. Never. This had to be a mistake.

Lily had been in tears, crying that they would catch the next flight home. She managed to convince Lily that she would take care of Travis. She would find out what happened and keep her updated if necessary. But under no circumstances were they to come back home. This was her honeymoon and she would enjoy it.

Sarafina, angry that someone called Lily, asked who told her what happened.

Her father.

Why in the world would Mr. C ruin her honeymoon? Times like this, that's what made him into a cruel and hateful man. These were the times she didn't like him.

Unsure of what was happening to Travis and the exact charges he was facing, Sarafina wasted no time getting to the precinct. Now, here she sat on a cold bench as she watched people come and go.

The precinct was busy for an early-Monday morning. Cops walking back and forth. Some alone. Some dragging along an arrest that looked plainly clear to her they were criminals. Women who looked like hookers. Men zoned out, hooded with track marks on their arms explaining why they were in handcuffs. One guy even had her backing far into the wall as he passed by, the blood sprinkled on his shirt giving him a killer vibe. Was that his blood or someone else's? She really didn't want to know.

Of course, she shouldn't judge any of these people. Innocent until proven guilty. She had to remember that. Because she would want people to do that for Travis. He was innocent. She needed people to believe that. Wanted them to believe that.

What she also wanted was the man behind the desk to answer her questions. What were the charges against Travis Chilani? How long was he going to be held? How could she pay his bail?

"Have a seat, ma'am."

That's all the blasted officer would say to her, even after repeated questions thrown his way. Have a seat! How in the world could she have a seat when her best friend's brother was probably sitting in a dirty, smelly cell surrounded by people who committed an actual crime? Like the man who had blood all over his shirt. She prayed that Travis was nowhere near that man.

Not for one second did she believe Travis committed a crime. Never. He was a kind man. Respectable. Better than that. He was a lawyer, for goodness sakes. Not a criminal lawyer, more dealing with corporate law, but a lawyer none-theless.

Where in the world was Mr. C? This was his son. He should be sitting on this bench next to her. Or better yet, demanding answers be given to him immediately. No one would dare ignore Mr. C when he asked a question. She wouldn't be wondering and worrying if Mr. C was sitting next to her.

He had the nerve to call Lily and tell her what happened, but he couldn't be bothered to come get his son out. Maybe he truly believed Travis was guilty.

No. Travis would never do anything against the law. She refused to believe it.

"Fina, what are you doing here?"

She looked up, the one time she had been staring at her lap, unwilling to see more disturbing people walk by, and she failed to see Travis emerge out of wherever they had him.

"Oh, Travis. What happened?" She stood up with shaky feet, wrapping her arms tightly around him.

He hugged her back, his body taut with tension. "How did you know I was here? You shouldn't be here."

She didn't want to pull away yet, needing to feel him warm and safe in her arms. "What happened? I've never been so scared in my life."

He was the one to pull away first, cupping her cheeks lightly. "Don't worry about that. How did you know I was here?"

"Your father, who obviously couldn't be bothered to come down here, called Lily. She called me in a panic, crying and upset. She wanted to come home. I talked her out of it. I told her I would be here for you. So here I am. What happened? Quit ignoring me."

He dropped his hands and took a step back. "This isn't the best place to talk. I can't believe he called her. She shouldn't be worried about anything. And neither should you." His face became hard as he leveled his eyes at her. "I don't want you here. You shouldn't be in this disgusting place."

"And you should be?" She leaned forward, whispering, "Did you see some of the people walking by? You are not like them. Why can't you tell me what happened?"

"Because it's not something I want you to worry about. Although, I do appreciate you coming down here for me. It's nice to know you care."

She lightly tapped him on the arm. "Don't be an idiot. Of course I care. You won't tell me what happened, just like that dratted cop behind the counter. Can you at least tell me this was a mistake? Is that why they're releasing you already? They realized how dumb they were to arrest you in the first place."

His eyes crinkled with compassion as his face continued to hold a frown. "My father may not be here, but he paid my bail. That's why I'm out. We'll have this situation sorted out soon. I don't want you to worry about anything."

"So it's a mistake?"

"Don't worry about it. I'll take you home." He started to put a hand on her back when her eyes widened with shock.

"Why is Franklin here? Were you arrested with him?" she whispered fiercely, trying not to make eye contact with that piece of scum.

"I was. Let's go home."

"Is Franklin going with you?"

"I'm sure my dad sent a car to take both of us home, so yes."

She took a step back and let his hand fall away. "I came here to make sure you were all right and to find out what happened. I can make it home okay by myself."

"Fina…"

Still refusing to glance at Franklin, who had the brains enough to stay away from them, she smiled at Travis. To offer reassurance. "You know he makes me uncomfortable. I'll get home fine. I might even stop for coffee. Call me later, okay?"

He didn't look like he was going to agree, his face a myriad of emotions that were hard to decipher, but he nodded once. "I'm doing more than calling. I'm coming over later. We'll talk. This isn't the best place for any sort of conversation. I'll make sure you get a cab."

She started to nod, then saw something odd out of the corner of her eye. Not sure if her mind was conjuring images to make her feel better, or if she really saw what she thought she did, her head turned to shake the answer no. "I have to use the bathroom. I'll be fine. Call me when you're on your way."

The pain etched across his face intensified. "Okay." A simple word that held such emotion.

He walked away, giving her much-needed peace, especially since Franklin followed him out. Of course, not without glancing at her and giving her a leer that made her skin crawl as if a million spiders were inhabiting her body.

Turning her head to the left, down the hallway that was suddenly vacant, she started to walk. She had no clue where the bathroom was located, or if she was allowed to step in this area. Either the officer didn't notice her move, or there was no issue.

Her heart started to race as she slowly made her way, glancing into rooms as she went, trying to find the one man she never expected to see here.

Dax.

Was it really him she saw? Or were her emotions so out of whack that she wanted to see him?

Having walked down the entire corridor, coming to a T, she decided to turn around and go home. Her mind had been playing tricks on her. That's all it was. She took one step, then froze.

There. A flash of his face dipping out of sight to her right.

With quick footsteps, she made her way down a new hallway, stopping in front of a tiny alcove where Dax stood trying to hide from her.

"Well, I didn't think this morning could get any more surprising. What are you doing here? Or are you going to refuse to answer my questions like Travis did?"

## 7

---

THE PAIN and heartbreak written on her face had Dax feeling like the lowest scum on earth. Seeing her in the precinct had thrown him off-balance. Trying to catch a glimpse of her, then attempting to hear the conversation with Travis had been a mistake. A deadly one.

Now she wanted answers. He was afraid to give them.

Not wanting to make a scene or be overheard by anyone, he grabbed her arm, pulling her with him until he came across a door. He whipped it open, stashed her inside, and closed the door quickly as he flipped the light.

A broom closet.

Great. He was stuck inside a broom closet with the one woman he couldn't get his mind to forget. Her scent wrapped around him, making him almost forget why they were in the closet to begin with. Then she spoke.

"Not going to talk, huh? Just push me around like the skunk you are."

"Damn it, Sarafina, what are you doing here?"

"No. That's not happening. You don't get to ask questions expecting an answer. I want answers first. You start talking."

She pushed him away, then pointed an accusing finger. "What are you doing here?"

"I can't answer that. I'm a jerk. There's no denying that. You should go home and stay there. Don't come back here."

"How dare you!" She advanced at him, hitting his chest, pounding on him like she could truly hurt him.

And she could.

Her hits didn't hurt with physical pain, but every time her mouth made a small cry of anguish, it crushed him straight to his soul. He did nothing to stop her barrage of hits, letting her get her anger out. He deserved nothing less.

"I hate you. This isn't fair. Men always getting their way, thinking they can avoid the questions, but expect them from you. Telling you what to do. No!"

She kept on hitting him until her face staggered into confusion, grabbing at his waist instead of hitting.

"Is that a gun? Why do you have a gun?"

She started to move his jacket at the same time he finally tried to stop her. "No, Sarafina, enough."

"Screw you." Struggling with him, she managed to snake her hand to his back pocket where she pulled out his wallet. A shove so forceful came from her that he had no chance to stop the backwards momentum. No time to stop her from flipping open his badge.

"The FBI. You work for the FBI? I thought you worked on Wall Street." Her eyes slowly trailed to his face, a mingled sense of horror and shame pouring out. "Everything was a lie."

Backing away from him, she hit the wall, unable to escape his reach any further. Stepping toward her didn't seem like a wise option, especially since her eyes zoomed back to his badge.

"Not everything. Listen to me, Sarafina."

Her head snapped up. "Oh, now you want to explain. Now you want to talk. Because your dirty little secret is out. You lied, Dax. Everything was a lie. Or maybe I shouldn't even call you Dax. That's probably not even your real name."

Throwing his hand out with exaggeration, he growled, "Look at my damn badge again. My name is clearly written in bold black letters."

Glancing down, she looked, but said nothing.

"My name is Dax—Daxton. I didn't lie about that. Ryan is my friend from college and I haven't seen him for almost ten years. I didn't lie about that."

Her eyes rose with tears glistening in the corners. "But you lied about everything else, didn't you?"

Sighing heavily, he ran a hand through his hair to stop himself from reaching for her. He wanted to pull her into his arms and take that painful look away. "I had no choice. Do you have any idea what kind of man Martin Chilani is? What the man is capable of?"

She started to shake her head in denial, but he wasn't about to let her ignore what she should've seen a long time ago. Like a panther on the prowl, he pounced on her, cocooning her into his body. "Stop looking away from the truth. You have to know he's a dangerous man."

"Get away from me."

"No." He braced his arms to her sides, boxing her in further. "You want answers. I'll give them to you. Anything you heard about Martin Chilani is true. You had to have heard things about him. He's a cold-blooded killer, a man with no remorse. We've been trying to nail his ass for a very long time. Witnesses always seem to disappear, evidence vanishing without a trace. He's not the easiest man to convict, but that doesn't mean we stop trying. We received good intel that a shipment of guns was coming in soon. Where and when remained a mystery. It turned out very convenient when Ryan needed another groomsman and that I happened to know him. Trust me when I say I wanted nothing to do with this. Ryan was my good friend."

"Was? He's not your friend anymore?"

"He wasn't exactly happy to cooperate with us. He didn't want to ruin Lily's big day. And we didn't. I didn't."

"No, but you're ruining her honeymoon. Instead of enjoying herself, she's crying, calling me that her brother was arrested."

His jaw clenched. So that's how she knew. "That information didn't come from us."

"No, Mr. C told her."

"Doesn't that tell you what kind of coldhearted bastard he is? Did she really need to know while on her honeymoon that her brother was arrested? I don't think so."

She tried to shove him away, but when his body didn't move an inch, a cry escaped. "Why?"

He brushed a tender hand across her cheek, letting it fall without holding its position. No explanation was needed for that loaded question. "Why didn't I keep my distance? Why did I give in to my emotions that you strung out of me? Why didn't I stay the entire night? Which one would you like answered?"

She sucked in a sharp breath. "All of them."

"I tried to keep my distance. You know that. Was I near you the entire night? No, I was clear across the room until Lily shoved you my way. When you're near me, I can't concentrate. Hearing your sweet voice, laughing with you, how was I supposed to resist that? I tried so damn hard to keep my distance, you have to believe me. I told you I was wrong for you. I tried to tell you."

"Fine, I'll give you that. You did. So why didn't you stay the entire night?"

"Do you think it was even easy leaving when I did? If I would've woken up next to you in the morning, I probably would've never left at all. Nothing can happen between us, Sarafina. That night should've never happened. While I should regret it, I can't find the energy to do that. I don't regret it. I won't let anything bad happen to you. Continuing anything between us would risk that."

"What makes you think I want anything more between us?"

Moving closer to her body, molding his frame perfectly to hers, he kissed her lightly on the lips. Knowing her exact reaction, or at least praying for it, she wound her arms around his neck as he deepened the kiss.

Wanting a lot more to happen in the tiny closet, knowing nothing could, he broke the kiss before all thought left his brain. "That reaction tells me you want more just like I do. But it can't happen. We need to forget everything that occurred here today."

Her hands slid down his back, falling limply to her sides. "I can't forget anything. I can't forget the look on Travis's face or the thought of him behind bars."

"What in the hell is he to you? He was arrested last night for smuggling firearms into the country. Weapons meant to be distributed to the streets. Yet, you sound like you're ready to defend him."

"He's not a bad person. I don't believe a word. He didn't do anything wrong. Now, Franklin, I believe—" Silence echoed between them as her face morphed into recognition. "What I told you about the conversation I overheard, that was the exact information you needed, wasn't it? I helped you. I helped you put the cuffs on Travis."

"I was striking out everywhere, not that I really expected to get the information I needed that night. It was a wedding. But yes, you gave me the exact information I needed. And you should be thanking your lucky stars you told me and not anyone in the Chilani family. Do you have any idea what he would do to you if he knew what you overheard?"

"Mr. C would never harm me. And Travis would never lay a finger on me."

He slammed a hand against the wall, making her jump. "Damn it, Sarafina, that family is dangerous. Martin Chilani wouldn't hesitate to take you out. He would kill you without thought and dump your body without glancing behind him as he walked away. Stop thinking you're invisible to that man...or his son. You looked very cozy with Travis at the wedding, and I have to admit, here at the precinct. I'm only going to ask you one more time, and I want a damn clear answer. What is he to you?"

"He is none of your business. If you think he's someone I'm intimate with where I would go home one night with you, doing the things we did, just to fall into bed with him, well, then you're a bigger skunk than I originally thought."

"Do you ever swear? It's adorable and painful all at once when you use words like skunk instead of asshole."

"You got the point. Don't try to butter me up with weird compliments." Her eyes turned down.

"Stay away from Travis. Stay away from that entire family. I don't want to see you get hurt."

"That's not possible, Dax. Lily is my best friend. Nobody in that family would hurt me. You're wrong."

Calming his racing heart at the thought of her inter-acting with them would be impossible. Yet, he couldn't stop her without taking her against her will and fleeing as far away as possible. That was crazy to contemplate. He did anyway.

"I'm not wrong. I'm so right that I even lied for you. Do you think I want your name associated with this case at all? Do you think I want your name to get back to Martin Chilani in any way? Hell, no. When my boss asked how I got that information, I said *I* overheard the conversation from Franklin. Not you, but me. Nothing will ever stop me from protecting you. Does that give you a clear picture of what you mean to me? I may not have known you long, and I may have walked away like it didn't hurt me to do it, but I care about you. I'm asking you, if you care even a little bit for me, to stay away from that family. All of them. Every single one."

Turning her head down, she barely hesitated when she whispered, "I can't do that."

"Are you going to tell them who I am? Because it doesn't sound like you care what happens to me."

"Your secret is safe with me. I won't utter a word to them, but I also won't stop seeing them. Lily is my best friend. I won't walk away from her. She wouldn't understand without me telling her why. You want your secret kept, then I stay friends with her."

"And Travis? You won't stay away from him either."

"I won't tell a soul, I promise, Dax. I would like to leave now. Please move."

Damn her for ignoring what he wanted. How could she think about interacting with Travis?

Refusing to let her walk away without one last memory, he kissed her hard, pulling her body deep into his. Like he hoped, she clung to him, knowing as well this would be the last thing between them ever again.

He kissed her like he was dying, like she could bring him back to life. Wishing that were true, but knowing his life would never be the same, he backed away and stepped to the side without warning.

"Good-bye, Sarafina."

No response but a nod of her head.

Within seconds, she was out of his life—again.

---

SARAFINA TOSSED her keys on the kitchen counter, then pulled out a wine glass and a bottle of red Merlot.

It was only ten o'clock in the morning, but that thought had no bearing on her mind as she filled her glass to the top. Anything to dull the pain. Anything to make her forget how foolish she had been.

Not only had she fallen for a man so easily, even letting him into her bedroom in one night, she had grandeur fantasies that he would change his mind and be knocking on her door before the day was over. How silly those fantasies had been.

He never had any intention of remaining in her life. She had been a means to an end. An extractor of information. Waking up in the morning alone, half of her bed cold to the touch, her mind still said he could come back. Well, there was no coming back after what she learned.

Walking aimlessly around the city the entire morning did nothing to clear her mind or change the facts of what happened.

FBI. A liar from the start.

Why had she fallen so easily into his arms? Why had he made it so easy? And why did he set his sights on her, like she would have the information he needed? She would've been the last person on earth to have any information on Mr. C's so-called operation. Because, no matter what it looked like, she had a hard time believing Mr. C and Travis were involved in any illegal activities. Franklin, now, she had no problem imagining him involved in anything illegal. He was a dirtbag through and through.

Slumping down into one of the dining room chairs, she took a huge gulp of wine as she rolled around the night of the wedding in her mind.

Walking down the aisle with Dax, sensing the tension between him and Ryan.

Of course, that made sense now. Ryan knew what was going on with Dax and hadn't liked it one bit. And why would he? He loved Lily and would never want anything to ruin the big day. So why did he agree? They must not have given him a choice. Or, more like, Dax hadn't.

Lora attaching herself to Dax like a leech, him eagerly soaking up the attention. She was a daughter of Martin Chilani. What better way to get information than falling into the arms of one of his daughters. Except she ruined his plans rather quickly when she averted her attention else-where. Why, when she was so eager to have Dax for herself? Because her father didn't trust him.

Sarafina laughed. Mr. C had great intuition because Dax couldn't be trusted.

Her least favorite part of the night, him extracting the information he needed from her. How stupid could she be?

But was she really that stupid? He made one point very clear and it was all true. He avoided her most of the evening. She danced, laughed, and talked merrily with a slew of people while he did the same from across the room. He hadn't made a point to seek her out, to dance with her, to even have a simple word with her once the reception offi-cially started.

No. She only started talking to him and dancing such a

sweet dance when Lily dragged her over to his table and shoved her into the chair.

Did that really say he tried using her?

No.

Did he purposely try to get any information from her?

No. She made all of that quite easy for him. She brought up the part about Lora. She mentioned the conversation she overheard without hesitation. He may have coaxed her, knowing he could possibly use the information, but she had given him the inkling there was something there.

As much as she wanted to hate him and blame him for everything, she couldn't. Part of the blame lay on her.

So why did he take her home and give her the most amazing night she ever experienced? There was no need to play with her emotions like that. That was the reason she wanted to hate him.

*I don't want to want you. But I can't help myself. Please, whatever happens in the future, know that what's about to happen tonight is because I truly care for you.*

The wine glass slipped through her fingers, crashing unceremoniously to the floor. The red liquid drained into the hard wooden floor, speckles of glass shattered around. Yet, nothing penetrated through the thick fog of his words.

A shaky hand covered her mouth as tears fell.

*I'm risking it all to have this one night.*

He did risk it all, didn't he? An FBI agent undercover, to what they believed a dangerous man, and he risked his job, his cover to have one night with her.

He tried to tell her it was wrong, that she should just forget about him, but she refused to listen. The attraction between them had been so strong, she refused to contemplate what he was trying to say.

As the sobs tore from her body, she couldn't regret any

moment they shared. Well, one regret. She would never have a chance with him. Such potential happiness ripped away from her without a beginning in sight.

The tears slipped down her face like a waterfall, beating her into defeat as they did. They soaked her to the bone, stripping her emotions bare.

Was Dax the one? Could the one man she had been waiting for to walk into her life and walk right back out without stopping?

Perhaps. She wasn't completely sure. What she did know was that he was special, kind, considerate, humorous, and so many other wonderful qualities that were marked on her list. Only one night and she could confirm that.

And good in bed. He topped that better than any other man. Scorched her body to the bone. Desire tingled in her veins, right then, to have him.

Wiping her face even as the tears continued to fall, she looked down at the floor to the mess she created. Another mess in her life that she would clean up and move on from. He gave her one glorious night. Locking those memories into the deep recesses of her mind was all she could do now.

Standing up and mucking her way through the mess on the floor, she decided that's all she had to do with life. Just muck her way through. These feelings were temporary. In a few days, it wouldn't feel like her heart had been ripped out and trampled to pieces. She would feel like a whole new person. Because that's what she did. Moved on after a guy tore her up.

She cleaned up the mess, took a shower to clear her head and the memory of Dax, which seemed nearly impossible, and curled into bed. The sound of pounding woke her up, making her realize she had slept all day.

Dragging herself from the bed, she grabbed her robe

hanging on the wall near her closet, and opened the front door to an irate Travis.

"What took you so long to answer the door? You weren't answering your phone," he asked, annoyed, shutting the door for her as he took in the state of her appearance. "Are you okay, Fina? You don't look well. You have no idea the worry you put me in."

"I was sleeping. The events of the day made me tired." Walking away, she knew he would follow her into the kitchen. Jeepers, he had walked into her house without her blessing. Just took charge. That was Travis.

"I'm sorry. You had me worried when you didn't answer. It's nearly five o'clock. Why were you sleeping?"

She grabbed a water bottle from the fridge, offering him one. Declining, he leaned against the counter and waited for her to finish taking a drink.

"I didn't mean to worry you, Travis. I guess I was sleeping so hard that I didn't hear my phone. I truly didn't mean to worry you. How are you?"

Shrugging nonchalantly, he crossed his arms. "I'm fine. I've been told to take some time off work. I guess getting arrested doesn't look too good. I need to resolve this issue and then I can come back."

"Oh, no. Are they firing you?" She set her bottle of water down and almost joined him on his side of the kitchen, but Dax's words stopped her movement.

She had no reason not to trust Travis, but strangely, she couldn't seem to make her feet move and comfort him like she wanted to.

"Not yet. I'll be back soon. Of course, my father says this is the perfect time to quit and make my way into the family business."

His hair that never saw anything but sweet perfection

looked like a bird's nest as he ran a tired hand through it. It didn't look like that was the first time he had done that same gesture.

"You're facing serious charges and your father thinks it's a good time to talk business. That's not very considerate. You don't sound worried about going to jail. Wrong place, wrong time sort of thing, then? I knew you had nothing to do with something like this."

He straightened up from the counter, a dash of pride combing his face. "You believe it was all a mistake. You have such faith in me."

"Am I wrong in that belief?"

Ignoring her question, she found herself becoming suspicious immediately when he said, "Serious charges? You make it sound like you know what charges I'm facing. How is that possible?"

Why couldn't he just admit it was a mistake? *Duh, Sara-fina, because it wasn't.* Even feeling a slight suspicion creeping in, she still had a hard time believing Travis would hurt her. He would never do such a thing.

"I finally managed to get a cop to tell me. Smuggling guns into the country seems like a very foolish thing to do. I can't picture you doing something like that."

"Your belief in me confounds me. You have no idea what that means to me. Smuggling guns does seem very foolish indeed. I don't want to talk about it anymore. And I don't want you to worry about anything. This'll all blow over and go away soon."

"You sound very sure of that."

Laughing, with not much humor behind it, he said, "My father has a lot of money. I have retained the best lawyer out there. He assures me it will all fix itself soon. Why worry?"

"I'm glad to hear that."

"Have you talked to Dax since the wedding?"

Sarafina almost let the water bottle slip through her fingers as she started to pick it up at the same time he asked the dangerous question. Did Travis see him at the precinct as well? Why would he ask her that?

"Why would I?"

"You two hit it off pretty well. I thought maybe he was the one who took you home."

If he could be evasive and ignore her questions, then so could she. "Perhaps I didn't want to ruin your evening by you taking me home."

"So you said you were leaving with someone so my evening wouldn't be ruined?"

"Just looking out for your libido."

He laughed. A true one this time. "I do love you, Fina."

"I love you, too, Travis."

Taking in her appearance again, his eyes trailed up and down her body. It unnerved her. "You don't look like you want to go out. I was going to offer to take you to dinner tonight. For making you crawl out of bed so early in the morning."

Considering herself silly for not wanting to comfort him, thinking that he couldn't have been involved in anything, she walked up to him and looped her arm through his. "How does takeout sound?"

"Like a very good plan."

He escorted her to the living room where they proceeded to squabble over what place to order from. Just like old times. A comfortable sensation swarmed the room, making Sarafina forget everything that happened. After pulling out a bottle of wine, they shared a few glasses as they ate pizza, an argument that she won, and enjoyed each other's company like nothing bad had ever occurred.

Closing the lid of the pizza box, Travis rubbed his stomach. "Good choice, Fina. I will concede defeat in that small war."

Tossing a playful punch to his shoulder, she chuckled with delight. "I always win the wars, and don't you forget it, buster."

"You managed to take a shitty day and turn it into something good. Thank you."

Grabbing her glass of wine from the coffee table, she smiled. "You're welcome. I hope you resolve the issue soon. I hate to even think of you behind bars."

"Don't worry. That will never happen. Please, don't worry about anything. Would you care to join me for dinner later this week?"

The word yes teetered on her tongue. Why was she hesitating? Darn Dax for making her doubt Travis. "That sounds nice."

"Great. There's this new Italian restaurant that opened that I'd love to take you to. So, you're not seeing anyone? You're not seeing Dax?"

"I'm not seeing anyone. Why do you keep asking about Dax? There's nothing between us." She seriously wanted to know why he kept asking about him. Did he suspect Dax was working for the FBI?

And if so, what would he do about that? Hurt him?

That was silly. Travis would never hurt another soul.

"No reason, really."

She wanted to press the issue, because she didn't like how he kept inquiring about Dax, when her doorbell went off.

"Expecting anyone, Fina?" Travis stood up, his body taut with sudden tension and his eyes alert.

"No, but I'm sure it's nothing."

"I'll get the door."

He walked away before she could protest. Could it be Dax? Did he change his mind and come back? As much as she wanted that to be true, she sincerely hoped it was the opposite. The pissing match between them would be inevitable. Why did that thought jump into her mind? Travis was a friend, not a potential boyfriend. He didn't see her like that.

She followed him quickly, her face lighting up with happiness when she saw who was on the other side of the door.

"Dominic."

"Travis."

Sarafina rolled her eyes as the two stared each other down and pushed Travis lightly out of the way. "What a surprise. Come in, Dominic. I missed you."

"Ah, I missed you more, darling," Dominic said as he stepped inside, placing a light kiss on her cheek while giving Travis a glare. "I'm not interrupting anything, I hope."

"No, of course not. Travis and I were eating pizza. Just a lazy night at home."

"I think I should be getting home myself. I had a wonderful night with you, Fina, as always." Travis pulled her into a tender hug, pressing a warm kiss to her cheek that lingered longer than normal. "I'll call you later this week."

"Okay. Good night, Travis."

Travis slowly walked past Dominic, eyeing him strangely as he did. "Dominic."

"Travis."

Dominic closed the door behind him, flipping the lock before turning back to her, two hands on his hips as he gave her a nonsensical look.

"Start explaining. What was he doing here?"

**8**

---

PLOPPING DOWN ON THE COUCH, she grabbed her glass of wine and took a nice long sip.

"What, you're going to ignore my question?" Dominic said as he took a seat next to her.

"When you ask it like you do, then yes. I never did understand what your problem is with Travis, or the way you two always acknowledge each other."

She looked at him and said with a mocking tone, "Travis. Dominic." Leaning against the couch, she laughed mercifully. "Could you two be any more obvious in your dislike for each other? I don't get it."

He tapped his chin as a mocking expression adorned his cute face. "Hmm, let's see. Maybe because he's the son of Martin Chilani, a man I've never liked and told you many times, and oh yeah, he was arrested this morning. According to the newspaper, smuggling guns. Why would I like that criminal?"

"Dominic Chester, don't you dare call him a criminal again," she stated in her most authoritative tone. "I know you've never liked Mr. C, but you have no reason to dislike Travis."

"Sara, sweets, please take the blinders off your eyes. That isn't a good family. Don't you read the papers? I know Lily is your best friend, and honestly, she's a peach. I have no problem with her. But the rest of that bunch, bad news. I've told you that from the start."

She always liked it when he called her Sara, one of the few people who actually did. Now it made her wonder why he did. Most of the Chilani family called her Fina. Perhaps that was his way of distancing himself from them. Dax's words filtered in, mingling with Dominic's. Was she really ignoring the glaring facts in front of her? Were they dangerous people?

She found it so hard to believe when she had known the entire family since sixth grade. They would never harm her; she believed that wholeheartedly.

"Did he talk about his arrest?"

"Not really. I have to admit, he was quite evasive on giving me a clear answer whether he was involved."

He grabbed her hand, clutching with a delicate tenderness. "What does that tell you, darling? He'll skate the charges like his father does, but he's guilty. Taking over the family business it seems."

Her hand became stiff, the wine glass almost slipping from her fingers. "What did you say?"

"What part?"

"The family business part." It couldn't be.

"You like to ignore the things said about Martin, but he runs a lucrative business in the crime world, Sara. Travis, to my surprise, has never been mentioned in the papers...until today. That tells me that his dad is finally trying to teach him the ropes, reel him into the family business. Clearly, he needs to teach him better. Getting arrested like an amateur."

Or because she helped that arrest go down. The family business. Was that what Travis had been talking about? Did he go down to the pier that night, executing a piece of the family business for his father?

"What did I say?"

She averted her eyes by taking another sip of wine. "Nothing. I just don't like it when you talk about Travis like that."

"Any more of that wine left? Your insistence to ignore what's glaringly obvious makes me want a drink."

She laughed despite herself, nodding toward the kitchen. "Help yourself, cupcake."

"I think I will, muffin."

He let go of her hand, squeezing once before he did, and walked out of the room. No matter how many times they got into it about the Chilani family, they never acted like the arguments affected them. This one, for the first time, affected her. Not even teasing each other with goofy nicknames like they liked to do was making her feel better.

Could she be wrong? Should she avoid the Chilani family from now on like Dax asked her? He had seemed genuinely worried about her safety. Dominic's expressions foretold the same worries. It was simply hard to contemplate ripping them from her life. They were like her family.

"So, tell me about the wedding," he said as he walked back into the room with a full glass of wine, the bottle of wine in his other hand. He refilled her glass, setting the bottle on the coffee table, and took a seat next to her again. "You never called me. I've been dying to hear all the juicy details."

"Geez, what sort of juicy details were you expecting? It was just a wedding."

"Exactly. Weddings always bring out the nostalgia. Any cute men you met? Details. I need details."

"How's Freddie? I was thinking I needed a massive makeover."

He raised a brow high as concern mingled with confusion touched his lips. "Deflecting the conversation. So unlike you. And massive? A makeover, sure, to make you feel a little better, but a massive one. I don't think so. Spill your guts, now."

A heavy sigh released like the helium from a balloon, making her slightly light-headed. Before she lost her nerve, she told Dominic every sordid detail since the wedding night. Well, everything besides the part where she overheard Franklin's disturbing phone call, seeing Dax at the precinct, and his secret.

His deadly secret.

She may not believe Mr. C would harm anyone, but she wasn't willing to take that chance. She gave Dax her word that she would keep his secret, and she didn't intend to break that promise. Even to Dominic, whom she trusted with her life.

He clucked his lips as he digested every word. "I've never known you to be a one-night stand sort of woman. You've been waiting for him to call or show up again, haven't you?"

"Maybe. I know that's dumb of me, but I can't help it. He was amazing. Different, unlike any man I dated." She nudged his shoulder as a sly smile emerged. "Including you. There was something about him. I know it was just wishful thinking, especially since we laid it out in the beginning what would occur between us. I don't know. I guess I hoped deep inside that I was wrong, that he would see how great we are. I know now it'll never be possible."

"You don't know that. It's been two days since the wedding. He could still change his mind."

Not wanting to spill the rest of the truths she was hiding from him, she drank a large gulp of wine. "It'll get better. I'll get over him. Good thing I took a week off work after the wedding for some me time. Who knew I'd really need it to recover from another broken heart."

Pulling her into his embrace, he rested his head on top of hers. "Must've been truly serious for you to have to recover from a broken heart. You barely know him."

"I know enough. I can't say love was in the equation, but there was something very special. It stinks."

"It does. I see where the word 'massive' comes in. How does tomorrow sound? I'll play hooky from work and we'll make a day of it. Massages, hair, makeup, spa treatment, and shopping. What do you say, darling?"

She wrapped her arms tight around the best friend she would never let go of and smiled brightly as a spurt of happiness surrounded her heart for once. "I say I couldn't have asked for a better friend than you. Does Freddie have an appointment available? It's last minute and he's always a busy man."

"For you, he has one available."

For once, Sarafina chose not to argue. She needed this. Needed to feel whole again, wipe away any trace of the woman from two days ago. Perhaps that would help rebuild the gaping hole in her heart.

DAX WALKED INTO THE HOUSE, dropping his keys into the first drawer in the kitchen. Standing for a moment, he took in the bleakness around him. Dark, empty, alone. That's all he saw.

Turning on the light would erase the darkness, but nothing would fix the emptiness. He certainly couldn't bring Sarafina to his domain like he ached to do. That emotion had been burning through his veins since the encounter in the closet. The urge to nab her and take her far, far away from the city still penetrated every pore in his body.

He knew she wouldn't stay away from the Chilani family, especially Lily. He wanted to say he had no problem with Lily, but he couldn't. She was the daughter of one of the most ruthless men. She had to be aware of what kind of man her father was. Ignoring the truth did not make you immune to the consequences in his mind. Did that make Ryan an accomplice as well? If Lily knew, did that mean Ryan knew everything?

Dax refused to believe that. By the end of the wedding night, they had reached a truce in their friendship. He didn't want to believe Ryan knew many disastrous things about Martin Chilani. But he could, and that made him just as much of an idiot as Ryan because he didn't want to believe his friend could do that to him.

He grabbed a beer from the fridge and downed it in one long swallow. The taste did nothing to ease the pain in his chest. Losing Bridget, who he dated for over a year, felt nothing like this hollowed-out pain that surrounded his entire heart.

Taking a little piece of Sarafina had been the stupidest thing he had ever done. He knew she would taste like heaven, and she had. Like the most beautiful thing in the entire world. How could any woman live up to her? It would be impossible, he knew it. But wouldn't living with regret, not taking a part of her, be just as bad?

Yes.

He would've never been able to live with that regret.

While he knew it would take almost forever to move on, it was better to live with her small memories than no memories at all.

Grabbing another beer from the fridge, he walked to the back of the house, slamming his bedroom door shut. Sinking into the mattress, he tried not to imagine her next to him. A king-size bed that would be perfect for exploring, treasuring every inch of her body.

He started to grow hard at all the delicious images swarming his mind, relaxing farther into the bed as he let them take over. Why did he let her walk away?

Jerking upright, he felt for his phone in his pocket. Who was calling him so late? Groaning at the name flashing, his body instantly returned to normal, every erotic picture deleted from his brain.

"Hey, Sloan. Don't tell me you're calling me in now."

"No, but I am curious what you did all day. You weren't at the precinct, were you? I thought I heard your name tossed around by Colt."

Running a flustered hand through his hair, he debated for about half a second lying—again—to his boss. "I might've slipped in the back door. Did you think I'd stay away?"

"I guess not, but I figured you would've made sure I didn't hear about it."

Dax sat up a little straighter. "Only Colt heard, right? Nobody on the Chilani side heard, did they?"

"As far as I know, no. You're safe, but it was stupid. Your name has been tossed around a bit by Martin Chilani, however. Not because of the precinct, but from the wedding. He's asking around about you. I don't like it. It has me on edge. I'm afraid we might need to do something."

"Something? Like what? If my cover hasn't been blown, there's no need to shove me into hiding. I don't want to lose my life that I built here."

"I know this isn't fair, and that I'm the one who asked you to do this. I can apologize, but we did get his son. So, I'm having a hard time getting the word sorry on my lips."

"Yeah, but how long do we have his son? He was out within a few hours. He won't see the inside of a jail again. I think we both know this. They'll do something to save his ass."

"We'll see. We caught him in the act. It'll be hard to get out of something like that. But let's get back to the real reason I called."

"Give it to me. I can handle it."

After Dax hung up the phone with his boss, he wanted to retract his words. He wasn't sure he could handle what his boss just told him. Life wasn't fair.

Throwing the phone clear across the room, hoping it shattered into a billion pieces like his heart basically did, he tossed back the rest of his beer. Drinking himself into oblivion wouldn't change the outcome, wouldn't change the course of his future. But it would dull the memories. That's what he wanted. Forget it all. Every little piece.

## 9

SHUFFLING AROUND IN A CIRCLE, Sarafina tried not to blush from head to toe. "I feel ridiculous, Freddie. Must I do this little dance?"

"I need a full picture of you before I create my magic to make the perfect after. Plus, you look adorbs when you blush like that, doesn't she, Dom?"

Dominic tapped a finger on his chin, as if he were thinking with Freddie what to do with her appearance as she displayed herself for them. "Oh, yeah. Totally adorable. I think a flush of highlights to tone down the dark brown in your hair and bring out the sparkle in your eyes would be perfect. And a cut from your shoulders to your chin."

Her eyes bulged. "You want me to cut half of my hair off. What is wrong with you? I like my long hair."

"You said massive makeover. I'm taking your words to heart. You want a change. Change is good. Let's make a change. You'll look just as beautiful with shorter hair. Trust me. Trust us. Trust Freddie. What do you think, hon?"

Freddie brushed his long fingers through her hair as he mulled it over. "Like usual, my Dom is right. I can do a beautiful cut to your chin. Nice, angular, sharp. You'll look like a knockout, even more so than you do now. Let's get to it. No more arguing. You win the arguments with Dom all the time, but you can never handle them with me. Sit."

His long, pointy finger held no argument as he demanded she sit down in front of the mirror that always made her look a little too mousy.

"I must still be in la-la-land to not argue with you." She sat down with what she considered defeat and closed her eyes.

"This could take awhile. Are you going to keep your eyes closed the entire time?" Freddie asked with quiet patience.

"Yes. I'm too afraid to look."

Shaking his head as he shared a lovey-dovey look with Dominic, he turned her chair away from the mirror. "Stare at the fine specimen in front of you instead. I can't have you tense the entire time I work my magic."

Sarafina laughed as she caught the wink from Dominic and tried to relax instead. This was exactly what she needed to lift her spirits and forget about a man who would probably be impossible to forget for days to come.

Three hours later, she stood in front of a full-length mirror, wearing a new sundress that Dominic pulled from a bag she had no idea he had hidden, and a new hairdo that made her feel beautiful.

"Well...enough with the suspense. What do you think?" Freddie asked from behind. "I love that coral dress on you. Dom sure does know how to pick the right outfit."

Brushing her hands down the dress that hugged all her curves, she smiled wide. "He does. It's beautiful. I love my hair, even though you guys made me nervous about the drastic change."

The soft colors twinkled like fine sand under the bright

lights, bringing out her gorgeous hazel eyes that finally shone with a bit of happiness. Her hair, now up to her chin, had long strands bowing from her forehead to her chin, dropping in height as it trailed to her back. Angular. She always wanted to try the angular look, but was always afraid to try. Having nice thick hair, it worked perfect.

"I love it, Freddie. Absolutely love it. Like always, you performed a miracle."

He gave her a sweet hug, then framed her face with his delicate hands. "No, like always, you made it easy. You two skedaddle while I finish my shift. You're not finished with this adventurous day."

"I'm taking you out for dinner one of these nights. No arguments," she told him firmly.

"I look forward to it. Now shoo!" He waved his hands for them to get going, but not before Dominic gave him the sweetest kiss to last the rest of the day.

"So, next is some shopping. I think a few more dresses like this one would be perfect," Dominic said, wrapping an arm around her shoulder as they walked out of the salon.

"I'm glad we did the spa and massage treatment before my hair. I'd hate to ruin the beauty of it right now. Trying on clothes could ruin it as well."

"Oh, no, my sweetie. You're not getting out of shopping. Don't even try."

"Okay, you twisted my arm," she said with a boisterous laugh.

Another two hours later, they sat at a quaint café in the heart of the city, surrounded by bags galore. She should've known in the beginning of their relationship, when her and Dominic had dated, that something was off. He always enjoyed shopping with her, picking through clothes with a delicate patience, never foaming at the mouth that she was taking too long. If anything, he dawdled more than her.

While at times she was sad she lost such a beautiful relationship with a man, she was still happy to have his friendship. Surviving this downfall from Dax would've been impossible without him by her side.

"What is that crazy mind of yours thinking?" Dominic asked as he set the menu down on the table and waited for the server to come back with their drinks.

"That I had such a great day. Thank you. I don't know what I'd do without you."

"I have no idea either." He chuckled as his eyes twinkled with delight. "Freddie adores you as well. We're thinking about moving in together. Well, he asked me. I'm not sure I'm ready for that."

She lowered her menu as the surprise took over. "I've been wallowing in self-pity over a man I barely know and you've been keeping this monstrous of a thing hidden from me. What is wrong with you? When did this happen?"

He shrugged like it wasn't that big of a deal. "A couple of days ago. You were busy with Lily's wedding and I was afraid to talk about it. He asked me. I froze. We haven't talked about it again. That's a big step in a relationship. You and I didn't even move in together."

Reaching across the table, she grabbed his hand and squeezed. "You also weren't being true to yourself. That's the only reason you and I didn't move in together. You're crazy about him. He's crazy about you. What part scares you?"

"The part where he sees more of me than he does now. What happens if he hates my habits? I can be a little messy, while he's more of a neat freak."

"I think he knows everything there is about you. Nothing like you being a little messy is going to scare him away. But if you're not ready for that step, then talk to him. Nothing is ever solved if you don't talk about it. He'll understand either way. He loves you."

"You're probably right."

She scoffed with merriment. "I'm always right."

Dominic lifted her hand, kissing the back of it with tenderness. "That you are."

Just like that, the issue was solved. She knew Dominic would talk to Freddy, and more than likely move in with him. Freddie could be very persuasive when he wanted to be, and Sarafina knew that he would do anything for Dominic, including getting his way when it came to him.

They ordered food, talked more about everyday life, a little more about the moving situation and who would move where. That told her that Dominic was already leaning toward saying yes.

"Oh, my. Is that you, Fina?" a voice screeched behind her.

Slowly turning around, she came face-to-face with Lora.

"Oh, my, it is you. Look at your hair. I love it. Totally frames your face much better than that other look. You look great," Lora crooned with too much excitement.

"Thanks, Lora. Dominic insisted I would, so I decided to take a chance." Sarafina stood up, gave her an obligatory hug, and sat back down, gesturing a hand to an empty chair at their table. "Care to join us?"

"Only for a minute." She sat down, giving Dominic a fake smile. "How are you?"

"I'm good."

A short and sweet answer like he always displayed to any member of the Chilani family, besides Lily, of course. He never did give any of them more than he wanted. Sarafina figured Lora expected him to ask her how she was, but he'd never do that because that would give her an opening to talk about herself. Something she loved to do.

"Very nice choice on the hair. Truly, it brings out your beauty so much more." Lora had no sense of personal space as she grabbed a handful of Sarafina's hair and tossed it around.

"Thanks, Lora." She swiped her hand through the strands Lora messed up and tried to fix it back to her liking.

"I've been meaning to talk to you. I'm so glad I ran into you."

Surprised by that, considering they only talked when Lily was around, she smiled anyway. "What about? Have you talked to Lily? Is she having a good time?"

"I have no idea. I haven't talked to her, but I'm sure she is. It's her honeymoon." Lora waved her hand like none of that was important. "I wanted to talk to you about Dax."

Sarafina tried not to look taken aback by the comment, or let Lora see the shakes that suddenly wanted to inhabit her body. "Oh, yeah, what about him?"

"Don't play coy with me, Sarafina. I saw you leave with him the night of the wedding."

She wanted to lie through her teeth, sort of how she evaded the question with Travis. Lora was different, more brutal than Travis would ever be. Lying wouldn't go over well with her.

"We shared a cab."

Lora leaned forward, the intrigue written all over. "Really? That's all?"

"Of course. Why would there be anything else? I swore he was into you way more than me."

"I thought so, too." She giggled, making that statement like it would be ridiculous a man would want another woman over her. "Of course, Daddy wasn't happy about that for whatever reason." Lora rolled her eyes in disgust. "So, by any chance, did the cab drop him off first?"

"Are you trying to find him, Lora? Do you think I know where to find him?"

"I was hoping. I wasn't sure if there was something between you two and didn't want to intrude."

Sarafina wanted to laugh at that notion. Lora would snatch him away, regardless of her feelings, if that's what she wanted. And clearly, she wanted Dax. Too bad she would never have him. Not even Sarafina could have him.

"There's nothing between us. I'm sorry to say the cab dropped me off first. I have no idea where he went afterwards."

"Damn. Well, here's where my next favor comes in. You know Lily and I don't always get along, so I thought it might go over better if you maybe called her and had her ask Ryan for his number. Would you be a doll and do that for me?"

Sarafina was literally too shocked to form any words, knowing Lora wanted her to call Lily right this second while she was on her honeymoon. That's how selfish she was.

"Gosh, Lora, she'd loved to do that for you when Lily gets back from her honeymoon. Wouldn't you, Sara?" Dominic piped in before Sarafina could figure a way out of this predicament.

Knowing how it looked, Lora placed a hand over her chest with feigned innocence. "Of course, after her honeymoon. I wouldn't want to ruin her vacation like that. So you don't mind asking her when she gets back?"

"I don't mind. But if your father didn't want you to pursue him, how are you going to explain to him when he finds out?"

"Daddy doesn't know half of what I do. I won't let him find out. It's not like I'm looking for a relationship." She stood up, adjusting her tight clothes that left little imagination of what was underneath. "You're a sweetheart. I'll let you two get back to your meal."

Sarafina said good-bye, watching as her hips swayed down the sidewalk with lush exaggeration.

"I can't stand that woman. I have to say that I prefer Travis over her. And give me a break. Her father knows everything. Is she really that delusional?" Dominic said, breaking her out of her trance of watching Lora walk away.

She turned back toward him, taking a drink of her lemonade to get her bearings in order. "I think she truly believes Mr. C is clueless. But I agree with you, he knows everything. She won't be able to hide that sort of thing from him, regardless of what she thinks."

"What are you going to do?" He reached for her hand, knowing how difficult that had been for her.

Without telling Dominic the entire truth about Dax, she gave him the best answer she could. "I'll ask Lily to appease Lora and let Dax handle his own problems. He was only being nice to her that night. He has no problem staying away from me. I'm sure he won't have a problem staying away from her."

"He's an idiot for staying away from you. And that tells me you deserve better."

Nodding like she agreed with him, she knew nothing would ever be better. Dax had set the standards high, making it nearly impossible for another man to take his place. He wasn't an idiot. He was her hero, protecting her from any possible harm. How could she hate him for that?

Simple. She didn't.

Except, she did miss him.

## 10

A KNOCK on her front door at ten o'clock that night sent a million B-rated scenarios through her mind. Who could possibly be at her door this late?

Sarafina stood frozen on the stairs. Normally, a simple knock on her door at any time of the day wouldn't have her in such a quandary. With all the crazy havoc going on in her life, it suddenly made her rethink who could be standing on the other side.

Another knock sounded. Quiet. Non-threatening. Perhaps she was creating a situation. It had to be a friend stopping by, or a neighbor in need of assistance for something mundane. People knocked on her door all the time for help with little things. She never minded. It didn't bother her if someone needed her help.

Yeah, right. Her luck sucked recently. Why would it get any better? She slowly descended the stairs with quiet footsteps. Small creaks echoed in her wake. She walked up to the front door and glanced through the peephole. All the horrible scenarios vanished and were instantly replaced by confusion.

Swinging the door open, she put on the bravest, stoic smile she could manage. "What are you doing here, Dax?"

Making a show of glancing around him, he said softly, "Can I come in?"

She stepped back, shutting the door quickly behind her. He had searched the area around him as if he were afraid someone would see him. Mr. C surely wouldn't have men around watching her, but she suddenly didn't want to take the chance. Dax may have broken her heart, but she didn't want anything bad to happen to him.

"Now, do you care to explain what you're doing here?"

Withering in her spot from his heated glance, she was almost afraid he was going to answer her question by pouncing on her, claiming her body in one smooth move. She could only hope.

*No! Hands off. It'll be much better for your heart.*

"I'm sorry if I woke you. Did I wake you up?"

Propping a hand on her hip like she was annoyed by him continuing to ignore her questions, which she was, she tried to erase the image of him tucking her properly into bed.

"What did you want again?"

Two could play this game. She could answer with a question just like him.

A slow smile crept onto his lips as his eyes dipped in delirious increments, taking in her entire body. "Would I get a slap in the face and a shove out the door if I said I wanted you?"

Her breath hitched as she absorbed his words. "Depends. How long do you want me?"

Sick of keeping his distance, or maybe he was choosing to make his move, Dax closed the space between them and pulled her into his arms.

"Sarafina, I wish I could keep you forever. It was a dumb impulse to come, but I couldn't stop myself. I shouldn't be here. You should kick me out."

"Okay. Get out," she mumbled as her body soaked up his delicate touch, imprinting it to her memory.

"That didn't sound very convincing." Stoking the fire already igniting inside, his lips met hers. Taking his time, he slipped his tongue in, kissing her like he was exploring an uninhabited island for the first time.

Breaking away, pressing his forehead to hers, he whispered, "You should either kick me out now or I'm taking you upstairs."

"You're asking for one more night, aren't you?"

"I need one more night to survive a lifetime without you. I thought I could just come here and say—" He sighed heavily, squeezing her tighter. "It's asking a lot, I know, but please, give me one more night."

"Until the morning?" she asked hesitantly, dying to know what he couldn't seem to say. Maybe after they found a little release, he would share his thoughts.

"I'll lose every ounce of strength I have if I stay until morning."

"You're just going to slip out in the middle of the night again? I didn't like it the first time, Dax."

"If I kiss you good-bye, would that make it better?"

Her rational mind told her this was utterly ridiculous. Tearing her heart into more pieces would not begin the healing process. She should kick him out and preserve what was left inside.

"Hardly, but I'll take it. If you walk out of this house without saying the words good-bye, I will hate you forever."

"We can't have that." He brushed his fingers over her

cheeks and through her hair, squinting his eyes. "You cut your hair. Why?"

"You don't like it?"

"You're beautiful. You will always be beautiful, no matter what you do. I like it. I'm just curious why you did it."

Grabbing his hand, she started for the stairs. "I needed a new me to make myself feel better. Giving you one more night, I might need to go back in for another makeover."

He paused at the bottom step, almost like he was giving her another chance to kick him out. "It was never my intention to hurt you, Sarafina. Believe me when I say, I'm hurting as bad as you. Why do you think I'm here?"

"No more talking. Are we going upstairs or not?"

Nodding, listening to her advice not to talk anymore, he followed her upstairs. Closing the door behind them, Dax started to undress as slowly as her. They stared at each other, the frenzy to get naked and in bed creating havoc in their bodies, but to rush anything seemed intolerable. Enjoying every moment, every second, seemed crucial.

She undressed first by one article of clothing and hopped into the bed. Joining her a second later, he hovered over her sweet body as his hand ran down the length of her.

"I honestly didn't come here for this. Seeing you again erased everything else from my mind. I swear the last thing I want to do is hurt you. Even in the beginning, I never meant to hurt you."

Cupping his face in her hands, she brushed her thumbs over his dark stubble and tried to keep a smile on her face. "I know that. Sometimes, getting hurt is inevitable, and you just have to take each moment slowly, to cherish it. I want you to cherish me now, Dax."

"I can do that. It would be my pleasure." Meeting her

lips, he kissed her hard, yet with a tenderness that made her want to shed a tear.

───────

HE SLID his hand down her body with a gentle stroke, finding his treasure with ease. So wet already for him. He'd probably never get tired of feeling her wet, unyielding, his for the taking.

That was the problem.

She wasn't his for the taking. Not whenever he wanted. Damn it, that's what he wanted.

His fingers continued to tease, play, and lift her to newer heights. Her sweet moans as they kissed urged him to stroke her a little faster, a little harder, her body moving sweetly to his touch.

He winced in pain when she bit his lower lip as her orgasm, one of the strongest she ever had, echoed in the room. He continued to caress her, never wanting the bliss to end. Her sounds, body writhing under him was a memory he needed to bottle forever.

"Oh, Dax, that was…"

He kissed her again, tenderly soothing his lips and her words she couldn't even finish.

"That was just the beginning, sweetheart." He reached over to the nightstand and grabbed a condom.

Sheathing himself with ease, he entered her in one deep stroke. She arched into his body, grabbing his ass to get him even closer. He stilled, taking the time to imprint the moment in his mind. He would need to remember every little thing because that's all he'd have to survive. Only memories.

"Please, Dax…"

He smiled as he stared into her gorgeous hazel eyes, at the pleading in her tone, the eagerness in her eyes for him to start the magic. It couldn't be described as anything else other than magic. No other woman compared to her. Maybe that's why he never fully gave himself to a woman before. They weren't the one.

He started to move slowly as that thought punched him in the gut.

The one. Sarafina?

Her soft hands ran up his back and slowly down again as she met each thrust.

Yeah. What a sad reality. She probably was the one. His one and only.

And he couldn't keep her. Couldn't have her. He could only have this night.

Life was unfair.

Her hands trailed the same path, making him increase the movements between them. Her touch drove him to madness. He wanted to possess, claim, and mark her body as his. She would know. Any other man to come after him would know.

She was his.

The heat in the room filled as it did between the sheets. Their sounds mingled as one. Their bodies as one. It didn't matter what way he moved, she matched it perfectly, never falling out of the beautiful sync they created.

Soon, the moment would be over. He felt it, sensed it. Hated it. He never wanted it to end.

Like that, it hit him. Strong, like a rogue wave capsizing an unsuspecting boat. The pleasure coursed throughout, zapping him into a peace he'd probably never feel again. She tensed beneath him, moaning deeply into his mouth as her orgasm fused with his.

Beautiful. Glorious. Heartbreaking.

He tangled his tongue with hers as the last remnants of the bliss still washed over him. Nibbling on her lip before pulling away, he kissed her neck softly, then rolled to the side.

Dax pulled her into his chest, stroking her hair as the silence filled the room. Not an uncomfortable silence either. One filled with peace and understanding. How was that possible after the mind-blowing sex they just experienced?

Peace, sure.

Understanding. Nothing about this could be understood. He hated himself for falling weak and coming over here. While he didn't regret the moment they shared, he still felt like a weasel taking it from her.

Without warning, he unwrapped himself from her and ventured to the bathroom to dispose of the condom. And if he was being honest with himself, to regain his composure. What they just experienced was too much. Too much of everything. Too much of a good thing. Something he wanted to experience every day of his life.

Washing his hands slowly, he hesitated to go back to the bed. But if this would be his last time with her. He needed to cherish every moment, no matter how much it hurt. He dried his hands and then climbed back in bed, pulling her into his arms as if he never left in the first place.

They lay in silence. Until her beautiful voice punctured the quiet. "It felt like you wanted to tell me something when you came over. Care to tell me now?"

Her voice, although spoken in a sweet whisper, rang loudly in his ears as if she had shouted. "Nothing important. Nothing that I want to talk about and ruin this moment."

Lifting her head, she gazed into his eyes. "That's very

contradictory. It's not important, yet you don't want to ruin this moment, therefore it's something slightly important."

His initial impulse had been to come over and lay his heart on the line, spill his guts on everything that was about to happen. The moment he saw her, the words on the tip of his tongue, he couldn't go through with it. Images flashed like a streak of lightning on her world being upturned, making it impossible to speak any of the words. He still couldn't.

"I missed you."

Cocking an eyebrow, she waited for him to say more.

"I'm sorry for lying."

Tilting her head slightly, she pursed her lips like she was wondering if that was really what he intended to say.

"You're the most beautiful woman I've ever met, inside and out. I wish like hell I would've met you under different circumstances...but I didn't. As much as I would love something to develop between us, it would never work. I would never risk your safety or ruin your life in any way to try to make it work."

There. He gave her part of what he wanted to say without actually giving her the entire truth.

"I don't think—"

He shoved a finger over her lips. "If you're about to say anything about Martin Chilani, stop. I won't listen to any of your naivety. He's a dangerous man. You need to start believing that."

Rolling away from him, she sat up as her face fell into a deep frown. "That was a little harsh."

Sitting up as well, he tried to keep his temper in check. Getting angry with her wouldn't solve anything. Not to mention, it would ruin the little time he had left with her.

"I didn't mean to make it sound like that, but you have to

understand what kind of man he is. Constantly sticking up for him, especially with me, isn't doing yourself any favors."

"Not seeing my side of things isn't doing yourself any favors."

Running a shaky hand over his face, muffling a groan, he turned toward her. "Can we not argue about this? I want to enjoy this night with you. This..." he said, waving his hand between them, "this disagreement won't even matter tomorrow. I'll be gone. You're going to do what you want to do, regardless of how I feel or what I tell you. You've seen Travis, haven't you?"

"You can say what you want about Mr. C, but Travis is off-limits. He is a good man. I don't care if you arrested him. It's his first arrest for anything, and he's never been in trouble before."

"Do you hear yourself? It's okay that he got arrested for arms dealing because it's his first offense," he said with a mocking voice close to hers. "And you didn't answer my question."

She poked him in the chest with an angry finger. "Well, it didn't sound like you answered my original question. You avoided it by saying other irrelevant things."

"My feelings for you are not insignificant. So don't insinuate they are." Grabbing her finger that wanted to poke his chest again, he slid his fingers through hers. "I didn't come here to argue about the Chilani family. We'll never agree. I don't want to keep fighting about it. I want to lay here with you and enjoy it."

Pulling her closer, his lips brushed hers as a small form of contentment swarmed his senses. Her next to him made everything better. It had since the moment he met her.

"I ran into Lora."

"I thought we would stop talking about any member of the Chilani family. I'd love it, actually."

A stroke of her fingers tumbled down his cheek as she stared at him. "I think we should talk about this. You'll want to hear it. Then we can agree to disagree. Although, I've never been a huge fan of Lora, so no arguments about her from me."

He wanted to smile at her sweet grin that accompanied those words, but he found it hard. Lora wasn't one he was too concerned about. Now, if she said that about Travis or Martin, then he would beam from ear to ear.

"Fine. Tell me about Lora."

"Pure coincidence I ran into her, but she would've contacted me anyway. She knows I left with you the night of the wedding." She put a finger to his lips to stop any interruption, adding in a shake of her head as well to keep quiet. "I told her we shared a cab and I was dropped off first and that I have no idea where you live, which is true. Mr. C told her to stay away from you, and Lora's never been one to listen very well. When she wants something, she wants it. End of story."

He swiped a hand through her hair as he waited patiently for her to continue, although he had a bad feeling where this was going.

"She wants me to ask Lily to ask Ryan for your number. She wanted you at the wedding and still intends to have you. She thinks she can hide it from her dad. Mr. C misses nothing, especially when it comes to his kids."

"The only person who can have me is you. I hope you know that." Adding a kiss to that statement to make it more real, he leaned back. "Call Lily. You were worried about what to do, weren't you?"

"So you're going to keep going undercover inside the family? I—"

He broke her words by kissing her again. This time, taking his time to savor her taste. Swiping in with a smooth stroke, he tangled his tongue with hers. Every time he kissed her, he took the memory as a keepsake to get him through life down the road. He really had no idea how he'd be able to leave her. Running away with her sounded like a better option the more it rumbled through his mind.

"You have the sweetest lips."

"You're avoiding the question again."

His hand still laced with hers, he squeezed lightly. "Call Lily and ask for my number. Give it to Lora. You did your part, and I know nothing bad will happen to you, especially from Lora since she's an unknown. She's not on the business side of things, but I don't like the unknown. The best thing for me is to know you're safe. That's it. She can call me all she wants. It doesn't mean I have to answer. I have no intention of going back in the trenches with that family. Trust me. Do you trust me? I haven't given much to earn that trust."

"I trust you, Dax. Lora...I've never been able to compete with her. She's beautiful, rich, and just has this way with men."

"You don't have to compete with her. You never did. You were always the one I wanted, even when Lora clung to me. All I wanted to do in the limo was turn away from her and pull you into my arms. Self-control definitely became a new meaning for me. You are something special, Sarafina. I can't even describe it. I already miss you."

"I miss you, too." Flinging herself into his chest, her warm tears started to soak deep into his heart.

"Don't cry. Please, sweetheart."

Between her muffled sobs still pouring out in heartwrenching agony, she whispered, "Stay 'til morning."

How in the hell could he resist that request? He should. Nothing good would come from him staying the entire night. Only more complications and feelings digging deeper into his heart.

"If I had my way, I'd never leave again."

That didn't answer her statement that was more a question than anything else. He couldn't answer it, though, since he had no idea what the answer was.

# 11

DAX HOVERED his hand over her arm, brushing down with a sweep as if he could caress her. Touching her would be bad. Waking her up wasn't a choice. She would try to talk him into staying until the morning and he couldn't.

When he woke up ten minutes ago, the clock on her nightstand told him it was a little after three in the morning. A sign. If he had meant to wake up with her in the morning, his body wouldn't have woken up. Clearly, he was telling himself something.

*Get your ass out of bed!*

Of course, he still struggled with moving away from her. The thought of leaving tore him up inside.

Leaving for good.

He would never see her beautiful face again. Last night he had almost grabbed his phone, wanting to take a dumb selfie with her. To have a memory of her would've been heaven. At the last minute, he chickened out. He always thought selfies were dumb. Never took one in his life. Why prolong his torture? Having a picture he could pull out all the time would only hinder him further. It wasn't acting weak in his eyes not to take a picture; it was staying strong.

Coming to her home had been weak. He knew that. Pacing his house from end to end hadn't helped make a clear decision, only confirmed he needed to see her one more time. Even as he drove into the city, he told himself every time he took a turn that he should turn around. Stay away. Nothing good would come from seeing her again.

He didn't lie to her. It hadn't been his intention to take her to bed again. The door slamming in his face was the more likely outcome. Surprised as hell when she let him in only made his best intentions wither away. How could he not want to taste her again? Asking for one more night had been crazy, but worth it.

A few more memories to sustain him. Finding another woman as sweet, kind, and funny as Sarafina would likely be impossible. Memories were all he had now.

If he hadn't been glad about the magical night they shared once again, he was glad he had a heads-up about Lora wanting to see him. Why did life have to be so difficult?

He wouldn't be answering the phone when she called, not caring how rude it may appear. Hell, he didn't intend to let his boss know she called either. Decisions were already made, and he would stick with the plan. No sense in stirring the pot and changing directions. No sense in delaying his future torture.

Convincing himself to get out of bed was getting him nowhere but deeper into misery. Brushing a small strand of hair away from her cheek, his muscles stilled in pain as she shifted her weight from the light touch. She curled toward him, stretching her arm, connecting with his chest. A small sigh of relief slipped from her lips, her eyes remaining tightly closed.

Groaning with pain, he watched her even breathing, the way she looked so innocent lying there, utter peace etched across her face. No worries. No guilt. No torture.

No. All those feelings were reserved for him. Guilt for more lies. She would never forgive him again. Perhaps she would forgive him for not saying good-bye while she was awake, because saying it while she slept would have to do. He'd take that forgiveness, but she'd never forgive him for keeping the real reason for his visit to himself. Finding forgiveness himself was impossible.

Time to go. He couldn't lie here anymore and analyze his decisions over and over. It was done. Nothing would change the course of his life now.

Leaning over ever so slightly, he kissed her forehead, lingering his lips as he scorched the feel of her soft skin into his brain one more time. Her breathing hitched, but no awareness pricked her senses.

"Good-bye, Sarafina."

The words barely left his mouth. Gently removing her hand from his chest, he rolled out of bed with as little movement as possible. Watching her sleep as he dressed made every task harder as each second ticked by.

Cursing out the unfairness wanted to roar from his chest. Instead, he clutched the door handle like a lifeline tossed to sea.

"Forgive me, for everything."

Then he was gone.

---

ROLLING OVER, her arm outstretched, the coldness moved over her hand immediately.

He left.

Slowly opening her eyes, the confirmation was clear. No warm body lay next to her. No male clothes scattered across the floor. Nothing.

"Darn you, Dax."

Sitting up, she rubbed her eyes as her head fell harshly against the headboard. This time hurt worse than the last. Forcing an ounce of surprise was useless. She knew this would be more painful, but regretting it was futile. One more day with Dax was better than none.

Being upset with him for leaving without saying good-bye was acceptable. How dare he lie about that? Why leave like that? Drawing one conclusion was all she could do. He didn't care about her like she did for him.

Sex. That's all this had been.

She figured she should be happy he considered her a good lay. Kept coming back for more.

Stretching her legs and moving to the edge of the bed, she paused. That can't be true. *Don't make it less.* He cared.

The energy last night, the connection created between them was too real and strong. It had to have been more than simple sex. He had to have cared for her a little bit. Perhaps he cared too much and couldn't stand to say good-bye. That excuse sounded much better than the first. She would stick with that one.

Getting ready for the day, especially since she had nothing planned, took longer than normal. Standing under the spray of water, not to absolve his touch from her skin, but too afraid to face the day, had left her like a wrinkled prune.

After having two cups of coffee, debating on a third, a knock sounded on the door. Hope sprang like a geyser reaching for the sky. Perhaps he came back. Not an ounce of foolishness touched her—he had come back last night. She never expected that in a million years. Of course, the guilt of leaving without a good-bye was so strong he couldn't stay away. Wishful thinking. That's all that was.

Wanting to be surprised, she flung open the door without looking to see who it was first. She tried to keep the shock and pain out of her expression as a small, tired smile appeared.

"Travis, what a lovely surprise. I was having some coffee. Come on in."

Travis walked in, kissing her lightly on the cheek before she closed the door behind him.

"I hope I'm not intruding."

"Not at all. I always like company." Waving her hand, she gestured for him to follow her to the kitchen.

Pouring another cup of coffee, she handed him a mug as they took a seat at her kitchen table. "How are you doing?"

Reaching out his hand, he grabbed hers gently. "I was wondering the same thing about you."

"Me? I'm great. Why would you think something is wrong?"

Shrugging, his face lit up a little more as he took in her appearance. Hair still a little damp and only combed through once, it was hard to see the new highlights, but the drastic cut was clearly visible.

"You cut your hair. I like it. It seems impossible that you could be more beautiful than you were before."

Blushing from the sudden compliment from him, she pulled her hand away and swiped it through her wet locks. "Thank you. Dominic convinced me."

"How is good ol' Dominic?"

"Why don't you two ever hide your displeasure for each other? Why don't you like him?"

"Why would I like a man that broke your heart? I haven't liked him since that day."

"Strange. I never got the impression you liked him from the beginning. He can't help who he is. I don't hate him for that. I can't."

"I know. That's one of the beautiful things about you. Your forgiveness and your kindness. You're the perfect woman."

Something in his eyes sparked an emotion she wasn't sure she wanted to decipher. Ignoring it, she laughed. "I'm far from perfect, I assure you. Now, tell me how you are. What are you doing today?"

"Hiding. I just want to rewind the last few days like they never happened."

Needing her space earlier, but now concerned, she reached for his hand. "Hiding? Are the police looking for you?"

His eyes had been downcast, suddenly shooting up with shock. "No. Definitely not. If they were, I would never put you in the middle. I'm trying to avoid my dad. We haven't been seeing eye to eye lately. I needed some air from him. You popped into my head and I thought I'd say hi."

"Good. You had me worried for a second." Squeezing his hand in reassurance, she tried to ignore the voice of Dax ringing in her head. *Don't trust him.* "Is there anything I can do to help? If you want to talk about it, feel free."

Bringing her hand to his mouth, lightly kissing it, he shook his head. "I want to forget about him right now. Have you eaten? I'd like to take you out for a bite to eat. We can have brunch."

Tossing the decision around in her head, Dax's voice popping in, she smiled. "I'd like that. Give me a few minutes to change and fix my hair."

Travis stood up with her, sweeping a lock of hair behind her ear. "You're beautiful as you are. Just thought I'd say that."

Offering another smile instead of words, she quickly went upstairs to change. He seemed to be doing that a lot more lately, complimenting her. Each time he did, it made her more and more confused. Uncomfortable, even.

He was just being nice. Typical Travis, that's all. Nothing more. Walking to her closet, she grabbed a light-colored sundress and tossed it onto her bed as she grabbed a different bra that would go better with that outfit. Turning back toward the bed, memories of last night assaulted her.

Dax would hate to know she was leaving with Travis. Part of her suddenly hated it. She trusted Travis. She really did, but Dax's words kept inching further and further into her mind. Could she trust him? He had been arrested for a dangerous crime.

Quickly changing and rushing to the bathroom, she dried her hair as fast as she could. Combing the tangles created from the blow dryer, she then grabbed a headband and slipped it on.

What was going on lately?

"Lily, I need you."

Resting her hands on the counter, she stared until her eyes glossed over into oblivion. She needed her best friend back home, but she couldn't possibly talk to her about Travis, her brother, or Dax, the man trying to take down her family.

Talking to Dominic wasn't an option either. She would never betray Dax's secret. If something happened to cause him harm, she'd only blame herself.

What option did that leave her?

Nothing. She had to keep her fears, her thoughts, her

turmoil all to herself. Surviving it all suddenly seemed impossible.

"Darn you, Dax."

Looking up into the mirror, she saw her future. Nothing but loneliness and fear.

Lonely, because she'd never find another man who touched her heart like Dax.

Fear, because she was afraid of what could happen to him. His words were slowly absorbing inside and the thought of leaving with Travis seemed like a very bad idea.

"Fina? Are you okay?"

Jumping, she placed a hand on her chest and turned toward the bathroom door where Travis stood.

"Don't scare me like that, Travis. What are you doing?"

A tentative smile crossed his face. "I know women tend to take a while to get ready, but I've never known you to take a long time. I started to get worried when you didn't come back down. It feels like something's bothering you. Were you talking to someone just now?"

"No. Only myself. I'm still debating whether I like this cut." The lie slipped easily from her lips as she touched a few bottom strands.

"I can't believe I didn't say something when you first opened the door, but it really does complement your face well. Should I say again how beautiful you are?" He took a few steps into the bathroom.

"No need. I believed you the first time." Not to mention, each time he continued to say it, it made her more nervous.

"What's bothering you?"

"Nothing. I swear." Giving a small laugh, she decided she needed to throw him off a bit. Letting him know the real reason, or to continue to dig for the real reason was inexcusable. Dangerous. "I think that time of the month is coming. You know how women get."

Surprised and slightly taken aback, he turned a little red and looked away. "Right. Are you sure you're up for brunch?"

"I haven't eaten, so, yes. Let's go." Pasting on a smile that didn't reach her eyes, she looped her hand through his arm and steered him out of her bedroom.

She didn't want anything to taint the memories of Dax. Not yet, anyway. Time would eventually erase everything, but for now, she needed something to get her through the nights.

One decision was clearly obvious, though.

She had to slowly start extracting herself from the Chilani family. Not Lily, of course. Removing one of her best friends from her life would be impossible.

But the rest? No good would come from them remaining so firmly in her life. The entire drive to the restaurant she could hear Dax's voice pounding in her brain.

*Don't trust the Chilani family.*

For some strange reason, she was starting to believe it. Nothing new happened to change her mind, except for the total conviction she heard every time Dax spoke about them. Travis was a clever man, always very in tune to her. He would eventually see something was truly bothering her, nagging her until she couldn't take it anymore.

Keeping Dax's secret would die with her. She couldn't risk becoming weak in front of Travis. Because every time he glanced her way, she could feel the wonder in his eyes. He knew she was holding something back.

PMS. She was going to use that excuse today like she never did before and start to weave Travis out of her life.

It was for the best.

Her only option.

So why did it feel like a betrayal to a man she loved like a brother?

# 12

A HAPPY SCREAM echoed in her ear as tears wanted to fall down her face. She almost pulled the phone away to tone down the scream. "Lily, I missed you. Don't ever leave me that long again."

"I missed you, too. I needed to talk to you a few times. No more screaming from me, I swear. These last two weeks were the best."

Sarafina sank down into the couch. "I bet. Just you and Ryan. What more could you ask for?"

"My father not calling me about Travis getting arrested would've been nice. It was hard that first night to get back in honeymoon mode, but there's a reason I married Ryan. If not for him keeping me grounded a few times, I would've been calling you nonstop."

"Yeah, I thought that was pretty crappy of your dad. Travis is in good spirits, mostly. I don't know how the case is progressing because he doesn't talk to me about it."

A week and a half ago, she had been prepared to wipe him out of her life, figuring she couldn't hold back her emotions. Why she ever thought Travis would accept that without complaint was beyond her. He had already stopped by a few times, as well as called to simply talk. Thankfully, he stopped asking if she was all right. Apparently, she could play it off well that she was all right when deep inside she died a little more each day.

"I haven't seen him yet. We got in late last night, and I woke up a little bit ago. Yeah, I know, I'm a lazy bum because it's one o'clock in the afternoon."

"Trust me. Sometimes, you need a vacation from a vacation."

"So true. So, it's Saturday, and I'm totally last-minute on you, but what are you doing?"

*Wallowing in self-pity.* "Nothing. Dominic's hanging with Freddie, and I haven't done much but pick up my house a little. You want to do something?"

"I haven't officially grabbed all my stuff from my parents' house yet, and I want to firmly be Mrs. Ryan Benson. So, I thought, why wait? Wanna help me pack up the things in my room? Boring, I know, but it's like this infection crawling through my veins, and I can't get it out until I just go do it."

"Sure. I'm up for reminiscing. I'm sure a lot of that is old stuff from high school. Your cheerleading trophies, little notes we passed back and forth, secret pictures of the guys we crushed on."

Lily laughed in her ear, sending her spirits a bit higher. "Maybe we should trash the secret pictures. I'm not sure Ryan would appreciate those. But hey, you're right. A trip down memory lane. I'm totally in the mood for that right now. Do you wanna meet me there in an hour? I'll sweet talk Ryan into letting me borrow his SUV. I bet I'll have quite a few boxes to take home." Another happy scream pierced her ears. "Home. Can you believe it? I'm a married woman with a home."

Chuckling, she stood up. "You always had a home with Ryan. I guess officially being married makes it more official for you."

"Hell, yeah. Before it felt like we were just co-habitating. It definitely feels different now. You'll see when you get married."

"I'll see you in an hour. Be prepared to get sidetracked. I want details on your honeymoon."

"I have some really good stories." Lily giggled with delight and said good-bye.

Sarafina took the stairs two at a time as she rushed to change her clothes. Heading over to her best friend's house in her pajamas didn't seem like the best outfit.

Pathetic.

Finding the energy to get out of her PJs never struck. She had been lucky she even crawled out of bed. As she dashed into her bedroom, she made sure not to spare one glance at her bed. If she did, she knew every delicious memory of Dax would touch her.

A week and a half. That's how long it had been since she last saw him.

Not a peep. Not a word. Nothing.

One more night. He hadn't lied that time when he said those words. Secretly hoping that he would change his mind seemed so far out of reach with each new day that passed.

She thought the memories would slowly fade, wither, and die. Instead, her dreams about him played as if he only left yesterday.

Hoping that he was an anomaly, a two-night stand that could easily be forgotten, she couldn't have been further from the truth.

If she didn't immerse herself wholeheartedly in her

work or out enjoying her time with friends, he was on her mind. It seemed inevitable that she would never forget him. The only solace she found in his absence was nobody in the Chilani family asked about him.

Of course, she only had contact with Travis, but she was thankful he didn't bring him up again. If he had, she would have seriously worried that he knew about Dax's real identity. So, she knew Dax's secret had to be safe.

Now that Lily was home, Lora would be on her heels. The thought of asking Lily for Dax's number made her nauseated.

Giving that wretched woman his number seemed wrong, even with his approval. Plus, the temptation to call him herself would be immense. She wasn't positive she could hold back.

What would he say? Would he even pick up her call?

The answer to that last question had her choosing not to ask Lily for his number, even with the obvious repercussions from Lora. The pain would be intolerable.

Screw Lora.

With that mindset, she knew she needed a breather before entering that household. Making an impulsive decision, she pulled into her parents' driveway before heading to her destination.

One of the best parts about being friends with Lily had been the short distance between their homes. Sneaking out in the middle of the night and meeting up would've been much harder if they had lived farther apart. Less than a mile away, she could remember many hot nights they traveled together, giggling, soaking up a little freedom.

Stretching her legs first, she then made her way to the front door, knocking once, and entered.

"Mom. Dad. It's your favorite daughter."

A tender laugh drifted from the kitchen as a voice she missed filtered with it. "It's my lucky day. Although, you'll always be my favorite daughter, since I only have one."

Sarafina hugged her mom as she laughed with her. "Oh, yeah, I forgot that part. Where's Dad?"

"Golfing. Probably sweating deliriously. It's hot today. What are you doing? This is such a nice surprise. We haven't seen you since the wedding."

"Lily wants to pack up her room, so I thought I'd swing by here first and say hi. What are you doing?" Sarafina eyed the tray of cookies and the bottle of wine next to it.

"Well, I'd like to call it book club I'm going to, but why lie? We never really get to talking about the book we were supposed to read, instead talking about a bunch of nonsense."

"So, in other words, talking girl talk. Sex, hot men…"

Her mother swiped her hand in the air as if to tell her to stop, but the smile on her face and the laughter in her eyes couldn't be mistaken. "I will neither confirm nor deny. When did Lily get back from her honeymoon?"

"Last night. Now she wants to get everything she owns into the home she has with Ryan. Well, that's how she put it. She wanted my help."

Raising a brow, amusement shuffled back into her mother's eyes. "Or she wants to talk sex, hot men…"

"Stop, Mom."

Her mom chuckled, then wrapped an arm around her. "I wish I could stay and talk more."

Sarafina hugged her back. "It's okay. I was only stopping by to say hi. I might walk to Lily's house. Do you mind if I leave my car here?"

"Of course not. It's hot, though. Grab a bottle of water. Why would you want to walk in this heat?"

Shrugging, she walked to the fridge to grab a water. "I'll probably drive with her to Ryan's house. This way I don't have to worry about my car sitting in their driveway. Not a biggie if it sits here a while, or even overnight if I can't get it right away."

"Good point. Lock the door for me, sweetheart. I really should get going." Her mother grabbed the tray of cookies and wine with a tender smile.

"No problem, Mom. Have fun talking about hot men. Don't worry, I won't tell Dad a thing."

Her mother laughed, winking deviously at her, then walked out of the kitchen.

Sarafina took a sip of water before grabbing a granola bar from the pantry. The heat was brutal today, but maybe it would help erase her memories for a short while. And she didn't lie to her mom. She probably would ride with Lily to transport all of her belongings and didn't want her car stuck at the Chilani residence.

Normally, it wouldn't have bothered her, but Dax and his worries were never far from her mind. Distance, besides Lily, would be best. Even distance from Travis.

If only she could stick to it. Every time Travis came around or called, her worries slipped away. She truly didn't believe he would hurt her.

Locking up the house as the sweat wasted no time dripping down, she blew out a deep breath. Like old times. Nothing bad would happen at Lily's house. Absolutely nothing.

By the time she made it to the Chilani home, she was dripping in sweat and thinking what a horrible idea it had been to walk. Lily needed her to help pack. Now she barely had the energy to hit the doorbell.

"Fina, always a pleasure to see you. You look like a

bedraggled doll. What's the matter? Come in out of the heat," Ms. Stinner, long-time housekeeper for the Chilani family, said as she waved her hand for Sarafina to step inside.

"I parked at my parents' house. The walk sounded like a good idea at the time. I don't really think I realized how hot it was outside."

"You silly girl, it's very hot out. I have to check the laundry, but you head to the kitchen immediately and grab a nice cold drink of lemonade. Freshly made. Lily should be here soon. She called a few minutes ago."

"Thanks, Ms. Stinner. I love your lemonade."

She placed a friendly hand on Sarafina's shoulder. "I know. Like I said, freshly made." With a parting wink, she walked away.

Moments like that made it hard to believe the Chilani family was bad. Not that Ms. Stinner was a true Chilani. She was only the housekeeper. Regardless, they all made her feel so welcome, so part of the family. They couldn't be bad people.

Then her entire view changed in an instant. The angry voice floating out of Mr. C's office had her slowing her steps outside the door that stood cracked open a tiny bit.

"I expect results. The fact it took this long to retrieve this information does not make me happy."

Sarafina shivered at the tone of his voice. Unhappy did not begin to describe how he sounded. Furious. Irate. Deadly.

"Daxton Delcroy. I knew there was something off about him. FBI. Why am I not surprised? Find him. Take care of him. And Ryan, well, that's unfortunate. I expect results much faster this time. Do I make myself clear?"

Sarafina wanted to melt into the wall. Slapping her hand

over her mouth to muffle the cries that wanted to escape, she honestly couldn't believe what she just heard.

Take care of him? What about Ryan? What was unfortunate?

Dax had been right. Mr. C was a bad man. Taking care of him could only mean one thing.

Kill him.

His secret was out. She could only assume Mr. C thought Ryan had a hand in it as well.

Controlling the shivers overwhelming her body became impossible. She couldn't stand here much longer, but her feet were frozen. The sound of footsteps coming her way inside the office jumpstarted her into motion. Backing up a few steps, knowing she had no time to go anywhere else, she tried to keep her composure as she started walking forward without a care in the world. Like she hadn't been eavesdropping outside his door.

The door swung open and Mr. C stepped out. "Fina, what a surprise? I wasn't expecting you."

Expecting? Mr. C sure liked to expect things in a certain way. *Forget what you heard. Stay calm. Be cool.*

"Lily called. She wants to pack up her room. Looks like we're going down memory lane. She has a lot in her room left over from high school."

Mr. C laughed. "Ah, yes. Memory lane. Well, don't fret if you girls want to make it into a sleepover. Make it a true memory lane sort of thing."

Sweat trickled down her back. Left over from her walk, or the effort to not visibly shake in front of him? Who knew. But him making that suggestion made her think only one thing. He wanted Ryan alone, Lily free. Oh, jeepers, he was going to kill Ryan.

"Fina, are you okay?" He took a step toward her and touched her shoulder. "You don't look well."

A laugh bubbled out of nowhere. "I'm truly doing the memory lane thing today. I walked from my parents' house to here and I'm exhausted. Ms. Stinner said there was freshly made lemonade waiting for me."

He pulled her into his side and started walking toward the kitchen. "My dear, Fina. It's terribly hot out. That wasn't very wise. No wonder you look so pale. You had me worried there for a second. A nice cold drink should cure you."

"She does make the best lemonade."

"And if she knew you were on the way, I'm sure she made it just for you," he replied with a friendly laugh.

"She did talk to Lily. And now I'm glad. I'm parched." She laughed, hoping it came out sounding sincere. His hands were rocking her to the core, scaring her more and more as each second passed. Could he feel the trembles everywhere? And if so, did he think it was solely from her dreadful walk? She could only hope. Otherwise, she would be dead.

Dax.

She had to tell Dax. As soon as possible.

What about Ryan? Should she say anything to Lily?

Mr. C finally let her go as they walked into the kitchen and grabbed the pitcher of lemonade out of the fridge for her.

"Girl, you're here. You look terrible."

Sarafina twirled around, the relief plain in her eyes. Not that she would divulge to Lily why she looked so relieved. She made up her mind. Lily wouldn't understand. She might confront her father. That would be bad. Very bad. She'd tell Dax and he would take care of it all. Trust. That's how much she trusted him.

"I walked here. I know. Dumb. Want some lemonade with me?" she said, as Mr. C laid a hand on her shoulder. Not tensing from his touch took all of her strength.

"You ladies have fun. I told Fina if you wanted to make it a sleepover with a true memory lane experience, you should."

Lily laughed. "Does that include sneaking out to go to a party with a bunch of boys?"

Mr. C dropped his hand as he walked toward Lily. "Not that you two ever snuck out very well, but I suppose. I'll be in my office if you need me. Have fun." He shifted his gaze to her. "Always a pleasure to see you, Fina. Drink up. You still look pale."

She lifted the pitcher he had set in front of her and smiled. "I'll be fine, Mr. C. Thanks."

He nodded and walked out.

Lily grabbed two glasses and Sarafina filled them up. She downed one glass with ease, refilling her glass before following Lily to her room.

How could she ask for Dax's number? How could she pretend like everything was normal? She had to speak to him. Right away. Now. Immediately.

Someone could be on their way to kill him right this minute. Every terrifying thing she tried to drown out when he spoke about Mr. C pelted her senses. She believed him now. When he said he was a dangerous man, she couldn't deny it anymore. She could only assume he would want the job done right away.

No—expected it done right away.

Lily shut her bedroom door and plopped onto her bed. "Spill it. What's wrong? I can't believe you walked from your house to mine. What's up with that?"

Sarafina dropped her butt next to her and then blurted, "I need Dax's number."

Lily's eyebrow rose in surprise. "That's so unlike you to go after a man like that. Good for you. But what aren't you saying?"

She let it all spill out. Well, besides the part where Dax worked for the FBI and that her father finally knew and wanted to kill him—and Ryan. Poured her heart out, even the part where Lora wanted to take him away from her. Because that's how it felt. Not that she believed she could. When Dax told her Lora held no candle like she did, she believed him.

Trusted him.

Right now, she needed his arms to wrap her up and make her feel safe. Or maybe she needed to wrap her arms around him and keep him safe. He was the one in danger. Not her.

"I knew you liked him, but wow! Screw packing up. Let me call Ryan and get his number for you. You can do your thing with Dax, and perhaps Ryan and I can christen our house once again," Lily said with a giggle.

Sarafina laughed with her, but it didn't reach her eyes, nor sounded real to her ears. That was the best plan. Her father wouldn't possibly hurt Ryan if Lily was there with him. Would he?

That's the thing. She had no idea. But Dax would.

She needed him. Now.

She only prayed he would answer her phone call.

―――――

DAX GRABBED ANOTHER BOX, shoving his baseball trophies into it without any care whatsoever. Did it matter if it broke?

Why did he even care about a dumb trophy anymore? His life, as he knew it, was officially over. Done. Complete. Wiped clear.

He was moving to Hong Kong. Or so everyone would think.

Witness protection? Not quite there, but damn close enough. Or maybe he was; who the hell knew. His story didn't hold as well as his boss planned. Here he was, a week and a half later, packing his shit and just waiting to leave. His fake boss was sending him to Hong Kong because his cover seemed to be crumbling.

Where he was really going, well, Dax wasn't sure. His boss hadn't divulged that yet. He didn't even say whether or not he had to change his name. The unknown bothered him. Worried him.

Why should it worry him? It wasn't like he had much family to worry about missing him. His parents were dead. Ten years already.

God, it's as if it happened yesterday. Stripped from his life without a backward glance. A man with a temper and a gun. Greed shielding his eyes.

A bank robbery turned deadly. His parents, with five other hostages, taken from the world without remorse.

Ryan asked why he dropped off the face of the earth. Well, grief had done a number on him. He had taken his anguish and put it to good use. Joined the FBI. His only family now. They were being ripped out of his life as well.

Maybe that was another reason he couldn't connect to Bridget like she wanted him to. Connecting meant inevitable pain.

Or not.

He barely had a chance to connect with Sarafina and he

was feeling the pain. Almost as if she had been shoved from his life like a quick push off the edge of a cliff.

He missed her. Her sweet laugh. Her beautiful innocence. Her delectable body. He missed it all.

And he couldn't tell her a damn thing. Oh, he wanted to so badly. He couldn't count on his hands how many times the urge to see her one more time came over him. The number was too high to contemplate.

He held it, though. Seeing her again would only make the pain worse. Not to mention, he might actually take her with him. Kidnap her. Steal her. Bribe her.

Whatever form seemed necessary.

That wouldn't be fair to her.

So he stayed away.

A trophy slipped from his hand when his phone rang for the third time.

Probably his boss—again. The man hadn't stopped bothering him since he told him the fatal news over a week ago.

Stay home. Don't worry about work. Pack up. Forget about the life you had.

Basically, his words in a nutshell.

He no longer had a caseload. He had no life anymore.

So, yeah, his boss could leave a damn message. He didn't need to hear for the umpteenth time, "I'm sorry, Dax. I wish I didn't have to do this."

He was sorry as hell as well. The main reason: giving up Sarafina before he even had the chance to call her his.

Picking the trophy up again, he threw it in the box. Not a dent, scratch, or clink happened. His life was broken, but his damn trophies refused to break.

Figured. Meaningless shit stayed perfectly together.

Walking away from the box, knowing if he didn't eventually call his boss back, he might send the cavalry. That was the last thing he needed. They wanted to ship him away to a far away land. Fine! Then they could leave him the hell alone.

He didn't want pity, apologies, or hell, even moral support. He just wanted to be left alone.

Swiping his phone from the counter, he scrolled through the missed calls.

Yep. Two from his boss. No surprise there.

The last one, however, had him hesitating. Not a number he recognized.

He hit the voicemail button and listened with half an ear as his boss droned on in two messages just seeing how he was.

Fine, damn it. Quit asking.

The third message froze his heart, the pain searing him right to the bone.

Sarafina.

"Hi...Dax...umm...it's Sarafina. We really need to talk. Please come over. Please. I need you to come right away. Call me back." A slight pause. "Oh, and be very careful. Very careful. I don't doubt anything you've told me anymore. Please come. I need to keep you safe in my arms."

Safe in her arms? What the hell was she talking about? She didn't doubt him anymore?

She could only be talking about one thing.

The Chilani family.

And she thought she could keep him safe. More like he might have to keep her safe now.

**13**

---

DAX KNOCKED on her door for the third time. If she didn't answer her door in the next ten seconds, he would be picking her locks and be damned the consequences. She called, left that terrifying message riddled with puzzles and the fright in her voice, and now she wasn't answering the door.

She said to call her back. He didn't think that was very safe or wise. His panic would've only increased as he drove through the city trying to reach her. Hearing her voice, how scared she sounded, he wouldn't be able to hear it again. Not until he could see her face, pull her into his arms, and caress it away. If that would even be possible.

"Shit."

He turned to grab some tools from his car to pick the lock when the door finally swung open.

"Dax?"

Shoving her inside without a word, he slammed the door closed, locked it, and pulled her into his arms. He waited for no invitation. His lips claimed hers with a searing kiss. She was safe. Unharmed. His heart still wouldn't calm down.

Lifting for air, even though he could kiss her all night, he knew they needed to talk first. Plus, he really did need air. It all left his body when he listened to her message. About a dozen times, if he were being honest.

"What the hell is going on? You can't just leave that kind of message on my phone. Do you hear me?" He kissed her again, unable to stand the fright in her eyes.

"If I knew a simple call would have you rushing here, maybe I would've called you a lot sooner," she said with a short laugh after he gave her a breather from another hot kiss that should've told her how scared he was.

"Are you telling me that message meant nothing? You missed me? Damn it, Sarafina, that's not okay."

He dropped his arms and stepped back. She was dressed in loose black drawstring pants and a tiny tank top. No bra. The picture before him was very enticing. Too enticing. But he needed to keep his mind on track. Get in and get out. Coming hadn't been the best idea. Or safe. Clearly, she didn't understand that.

But the fright in her eyes. What was that about?

She wrapped her arms around her chest and shivered. "I did miss you."

"Yeah, I got that." He swiped a hand through his hair.

"You didn't let me finish. I called for a reason."

"Please, elaborate."

"Don't be mad at me. What did I do wrong?" She threw her hands in the air and walked toward the living room.

Willing himself to calm down, not sure that would be possible, he followed her to the couch and took a seat next to her. "You scared the shit out of me. Forgive me if I'm having a hard time staying calm right now. The message sounded serious, even though you gave me no specifics. It's what you didn't say that has me worried."

Clasping her hands tightly, she stared at the floor as she said, "I'm scared, Dax. For you."

The fear again. Her voice trembled with it.

Cupping her chin lightly, he pulled her eyes to his. "Why? Tell me what's going on."

"I went over to Lily's house today. I mean, Mr. C's house, to help her pack up her old room. I walked from my parents' house and made it there before her. I heard Mr. C talking on the phone. I heard him..." Her eyes drifted down.

He brushed his lips to hers, then dropped his hand from her chin and grabbed a hold of her hands. Prying them apart, he linked their hands together and squeezed. "What did you hear? Just tell me."

She lifted her eyes to his again. The fear was so strong he wanted to scoop her into his arms and whisk her far, far away from the city. From the Chilani family.

"He knows you're an FBI agent."

"Shit." He nodded and squeezed her hands again in reassurance. "What else did he say?"

"He told whoever he was talking to...to take care of you. Maybe I was naïve before, but I'm not dumb. I know what that means. I don't want anyone to hurt you. I never imagined that he..."

No more. He couldn't take it anymore, especially when the tears started to fall. He let her hands go, scooped her onto his lap, and held on tightly.

"No one will hurt me. I swear."

"You can't make that sort of promise, Dax. You're not invincible."

"No, I'm not, but I am a trained FBI agent. I know how to be watchful, careful, and fight back." He sighed heavily. "My boss was already making plans for me to leave. He didn't think my backstory would hold. Clearly, it didn't."

"Is that why you showed up the second time?"

More pain in her voice. He was the sole cause of it. "It was better not to tell you anything. I really hate it that you keep overhearing conversations, Sarafina. I swear... Does he know you overheard anything? If he does—"

She shook her head. "No. He doesn't. I don't think so."

"There's a distinct difference between *no* and *I don't think so*. A huge difference. I will not let anyone hurt you, especially that man. He's dangerous. I hope you're planning to stay away from them now. You better say yes or we'll be having a serious argument here."

"Lily is—"

"I don't give a shit what Lily is. Your safety is all that matters. I can't leave to go anywhere if I know you're going to be in harm's way. I just can't." He pulled her tighter into his embrace. She had to feel the terror for her safety running through his veins. The pounding of his heart. The queasy feeling in his stomach. The short breaths he couldn't seem to control.

"He mentioned Ryan's name. He said, 'And Ryan, well, that's unfortunate.' He wouldn't really hurt his own daughter's husband, would he? Please tell me he wouldn't, Dax."

Damn it. Ryan, too. His whole world was falling down around him, and apparently, Sarafina's as well.

"I won't lie to you. Never again will I lie to you. I think you know the answer to that question." He kissed the top of her head. "He'll kill him. I would like to think he'd never harm one of his children, but I can't say for sure. We have files a mile long full of shit he's done. Murders you probably couldn't stand to hear. When I say he's a dangerous man, I mean it."

"What about Ryan?"

"Don't worry about it."

She lifted her head and hit him square in the chest. And damn if it didn't hurt a little. A very powerful punch for such a small woman.

"That's my best friend's husband. Your friend. Don't ignore me. Don't ignore my feelings."

A slow grin grew into a delicious smile. "You have a hard punch, sweetheart."

She hit him again, although, not as hard. More playfully. "And you ignored what I said."

"Telling you not to worry helps me not to worry. You think I'm not scared? I am. For Ryan. For you."

"And yourself?"

He shrugged. Why worry about himself? Besides an aunt he rarely talked to, he had nobody but his work buddies in his life.

"What are you going to do, Dax?"

"Taking you upstairs to a nice soft bed sounds like a good plan."

"Dax..."

He kissed her slowly. Treasuring her sweet taste, the delicate, perfect way she fit in his arms. "You scared about fifty years off my life. I need you. Tell me you need me, too."

Her breathing became ragged and rough as she caressed his cheek with a tenderness that would've unfrozen his heart if she hadn't already warmed it.

"I needed you all week. I definitely need you now."

He stood up with her still cradled in his arms perfectly. "That's all I needed to hear. No more talking. I only want to feel your body next to mine."

Arm outstretched, the coldness traveled from her hand straight to her heart.

Again. He did it again.

"Darn you, Dax."

"Well, that doesn't sound good. What did I do so I can mentally prepare on how to fix the problem?"

She sat up straight. Dax stood outside her bathroom door, a sweet grin on his face as the sun shining through the window hit his feet, his hair damp from a recent shower.

"The bed's cold. I thought..."

He walked quickly to the bed, dipping to the middle, and planted a sweet kiss to her lips. "You thought I left. There's no way in hell I'm leaving you until I know you're safe."

"So there's still an expiration date?"

He leaned away from her, running a hand through his hair. A loud sigh escaped. He rubbed his jaw, rough stubble still marking his face. "What are you saying, Sarafina?"

The stress etched on his face. The question in his eyes. The way he struggled to say something, yet didn't say it.

"What are *you* saying, Dax?"

"My life...it's sort of restarting itself. I don't have many people in my life to make it a big deal. My parents...they've been gone for ten years. I can handle this. I would never ask you to handle it."

She scooted closer to him and grabbed his hand that wouldn't stop rubbing his jaw. "Meaning you want to ask me to make a new life with you?"

"You have friends and a family. A good job." He laughed. "Whatever the hell that is. I still have no clue."

"You're really good at avoiding an honest answer."

"Yeah. Talking isn't a strong suit of mine. Ask my ex-girlfriend. One of the reasons she's my ex."

She cupped his face. To soothe the pain she heard in his voice. To feel the roughness of his jaw. He could pretend to be so rough on the outside, but he was nothing but sweetness and kindness inside.

"She didn't know how to patiently wait for you to answer. I have patience."

Turning his head slightly, he kissed the palm of her hand. "What do you do for a living?"

"I'm a school teacher."

His laughter filled the room, as did her heart. "Try again, sweetheart. You're a horrible liar." His smile faded, the light in his eyes turning to fear. "Which makes me very concerned Martin Chilani knows that, too."

"Why wouldn't you believe that?"

"You have patience, yes. Something you probably need to be a teacher. But I just know. I can see it in your eyes it's not true."

"Interior designer. Or more like an apprentice, gopher, do whatever my boss says or else. I would love to own my own company someday. I like creating beautiful things. That's what I do."

"Now that, I believe. Your house felt welcoming the moment I entered it."

Smiling, his words lifted her spirits. She kissed him in thanks. "I didn't even give you a full tour yet, but thank you. It's early. What are you doing up?"

"Couldn't sleep. I was talking to my boss again for the umpteenth time. Ryan's still okay. There are agents outside his house, but I can't ignore it anymore. I have to talk to him. Take care of things before Martin Chilani does."

"What does that mean? Tell me the truth. Don't ignore it. The plain truth."

He squeezed her hand tightly. "I think you know, but for some reason you just need to hear it. Why?"

She shoved him hard, laughing, even though it really wasn't funny. "Dodging again."

He righted himself before he fell off the bed, laughing with her. "You punch hard. You push hard. You probably even lo—" His face fell into a frown. "Ryan has to make a choice. Mine's already made. I'm leaving. Starting over. He needs to make the same choice. Martin Chilani won't stop until he's dead. You don't cross that man and get away with it."

"And Lily?"

"That's Ryan's decision. I can't make that for him. She'd have to give up everything she knows. Her family. Her life. Her friends. He'd have to tell her the truth about her father. Do you think she can handle that?"

She glanced away. "Do you want to ask me to give everything up?"

"It doesn't matter what I want."

The bed dipped. Panic started to well inside as he walked toward the door. He was leaving. Just like that. Without even answering her question with honesty.

"Where are you going?"

He gripped the door handle. "The agents outside his house said Lily left. I need to go over there while she's away. I'll be back."

"But for how long? And leaving without saying good-bye again?"

He stalked over to the bed, leaning until he was inches from her face. "I've never left without saying good-bye. Perhaps you were sleeping, but I still said it."

"You didn't just now."

"Do you know how hard it is to leave you?"

"Probably as hard as it is to watch you leave, or wake up knowing you're already gone. I truly hate that, Dax."

He slammed his lips across hers, demanding entrance. Their tongues tangoed, danced, and promised there was more to come. That was a lie. He was leaving.

He broke the kiss, framing her face tightly in his hands. "Stay home. Don't let anyone in. I'll be back soon and we'll talk."

A lame laugh came out. "Like we just talked?"

"Real, honest to goodness talking. Your patience will be worth it. I promise. I will talk."

She nodded, afraid to say anything else. No lies this time. She could see it in his eyes. Although, she was nervous to talk now. In all likelihood, she wouldn't like what he had to say.

"Sarafina, I—" He kissed her hard again. Stalling his words for the second time that morning. "Lock the door. Stay inside."

He let her go and walked out of the room before she could offer any words of safety. He had to be careful as well. He had to stay safe. In her arms.

Darnation. He should've never left.

## 14

Ryan shoved his hands in his hair and groaned. Loudly. The sound almost mimicked an animal in agonizing pain as if it were stuck in a metal trap, imminent death looming when the hunter would arrive.

"I'm sorry, Ryan."

Ryan looked at Dax and swore viciously. "Sorry that you ruined my life, or that her father wants to kill me? Sorry that you were right and he's that cruel of a man? Sorry that he wouldn't hesitate to destroy his daughter's life to save his own ass? What the hell are you sorry for?"

"Everything." Dax leaned forward on the couch, clasping his hands. "How long will Lily be gone? I don't want to be here when she gets back."

"Can't look her in the eye, huh?"

"More like I want it to be your choice, your decision. Do you want to ask her to give everything up? Do you want to tell her what sort of man her father is?"

Ryan shrugged, sinking back into the chair. "Fina is absolutely sure she heard everything correctly?"

"Do you honestly doubt Sarafina?"

"She's the most honest person I know. The sweetest. You love her, don't you?"

Dax sunk back into the couch and shrugged. "Does it matter?"

Of course, he loved her. He almost blurted it out this morning. The terror running through his veins of leaving had almost sucked the words out of his mouth. Yet, he couldn't do that to her. He couldn't ask her to give everything up for him. What made him worth that?

Damn, her sweet, innocent words this morning. *Do you want to ask me to give everything up?* Hell, yes, he wanted to. But he wouldn't. She deserved better.

"What happened to you, Dax? You used to be full of life. Now all I see is a hard, difficult man."

"When your life gets turned upside down, it's pretty difficult to stay full of life." He leaned forward again. "My parents were killed in a bank robbery gone bad. Life changed for me after that. It's changing again. I'll adapt. I've done it before. You never have. This is your life we're talking about. Lily's life. Can you live without her?"

Ryan leaned forward as well. "Can you live without Fina?"

Dax stood up. He could barely handle the internal war raging inside. There's no way he could handle one out in the open.

"You have to make a decision. And quickly. We have agents outside your house, but I guarantee Martin Chilani's men are right in the mix as well."

"I'm sorry about your parents. I would've been there for you if I had known."

Dax nodded. "You were there for me. Trust me."

"I love Lily. I love everything about her. Her father's willing to kill me without so much as blinking an eye. I find it hard to believe he wouldn't hurt her for some reason."

"What are you saying?"

Ryan stood up, his stance a little wobbly. "I'm saying I need my best friend here when I ask my wife to run away with me because her father wants to kill me."

---

Sarafina paced the living room as the clock ticked mutinously away.

Two hours. He had been gone for two long, terrifying hours already. No phone call. No word. Nothing.

He was a trained agent. She knew this. He could take care of himself. He had for his entire life. But the thought something terrible happened wouldn't go away.

She felt like the worst friend ever as well. Lily had called an hour ago wanting to pack up her room again. She was already at her parents' house. Having to utter the word no had been difficult. Heartwrenching.

How could she tell her best friend that her father wanted to kill Dax and her husband? How could she live the rest of her life looking Lily in the eye and keep that from her?

Maybe she wouldn't have to. Ryan loved Lily. He loved her so much. It was hard to imagine he wouldn't ask her to go with him. Wherever that would be.

Would Dax ask her to go with him? And if he did, what would she say?

She had a family. Not a huge family by some people's standards, but big enough. A brother. Her parents. A sprinkle of aunts, uncles, and cousins. Her best friend Dominic. Could she leave them for one person? A person she met less than two weeks ago. A person who stole her heart away with little effort.

She blew a deep breath. Talking was overrated. No wonder Dax didn't like to talk. A person had to dig deep and face the truth.

One man, or an entire family? That was the decision she faced. What a terrifying decision.

A loud ring echoed throughout her house. She jumped, nearly tripping over her coffee table.

Dax.

He finally made it back.

She rushed to the door and jumped again when she saw Travis standing on her doorstep through the peephole.

Oh, darnation.

Dax said not to let anyone in. How in the world could she turn him away? He would never understand or take no for an answer.

Deep breath. Stay calm. Show no fear.

Yeah, right. He'd probably see through it in a minute.

The doorbell rang again.

Another deep breath. She tore open the door with the friendliest smile she could manage.

"Hey, Travis."

He smiled his sweet, gentle smile he always gave her. "Hey, Fina. Can we come in?"

"We?" She looked behind him and nearly dropped her façade, showing her true fear. "Hi, Mr. C. What a surprise. Come in."

She stepped aside to let them in, knowing it would be impossible to turn them away. Why was Mr. C with Travis? He had never, not once, visited her house before.

"What a beautiful home you have, Fina. Truly displays your wonderful personality." Mr. C looked at her surroundings as he stepped inside and closed the door. She tried not to visibly shake.

"Thanks. It's what I do." She laughed. "Do you guys want coffee or something?"

"No, we're fine." Mr. C gestured toward her living room. "Let's chat."

She nodded and nearly jumped with surprise when Travis laid a hand on her lower back. He lowered his mouth near her ear as they walked into the living room and whispered, "It's okay. My dad said he wanted to talk to you about something and asked that I come with. Don't look so scared. It'll be okay."

She truly wanted to believe that. But Travis's words didn't comfort her. His hand on her gave no relief. Something bad was about to happen. More talk she didn't want to have.

Dax was right. She was a horrible liar. Mr. C knew the truth. He knew she heard everything. She would die today. The question that puzzled her: how could Travis come with and let it happen?

She was the dumbest person alive to have trusted one member of the Chilani family. Except for Lily. She trusted her with her life.

"Lily stopped by this morning," Mr. C said, still standing in the threshold of the living room while her and Travis took a spot near the coffee table. "I heard her talking to you. She wanted to know if you called Dax. Now, Fina, I would like to know why you would want to talk to him."

Oh, no. Perhaps she couldn't trust Lily either.

Travis's hand dropped from her back. He took a step away from her as his face fell into a deep frown.

"I don't have all day. Answer my question now." Mr. C's lips grew into a thin line.

He only used that tone of voice when he meant business.

She was a dead woman. She only hoped Dax didn't come back while they were still here. He didn't deserve to die as well.

---

"Ryan, I'm back."

Lily's voice floated into the living room where Dax and Ryan still sat. They hadn't moved much. Barely talked. When they did, it had been about mundane things. Dax understood why Ryan wanted him here, but his feet itched to leave. He worried about Sarafina. The more he worried, the more he came to realize he might not be able to leave without her.

"In the living room, Lily." Ryan glanced at him and took a deep breath.

Ryan stood up from the chair and pulled her into his arms as soon as she was in reaching distance. Dax stood up as well and waited for them to say hello in the most delicious way. With a kiss.

That's what he wanted. With Sarafina. He wanted to come home after a long day and pull her into his arms and kiss her as if she were the only thing that mattered.

Lily's face bloomed a deep red when she finally realized he was in the room as well. "Hi, Dax. What brings you by?"

"Probably something you won't like."

Ryan glared at him and hugged her tightly to his side. "Let's sit, Lily."

She stepped away from him and frowned. "No. We won't sit. He's mad because you gave me his number to give to Fina. You don't deserve her."

*Ain't that the truth.* She hit the nail on the head. He didn't deserve her. "I'm not mad."

"Well, what won't I like?" She crossed her arms, glancing between the two like they better stop messing with her as if they had been.

Maybe he shouldn't have answered her original question so abruptly.

"Dax is an FBI agent. He's not in finance." Ryan groaned and grabbed her hands. "Travis was arrested recently..."

She whipped her eyes to him, yet continued to let Ryan hold her hands. "Old news, but I guess something you obviously had to do with."

"Our main target was your father, actually. Not my fault Travis went in his place."

Ryan glared at him again. "Dax doesn't have much tact when it comes to talking, sweetheart. Look at me."

"Why was he at our wedding?" Lily refused to look at Ryan.

"Are you naïve, Lily? Or do you just like to ignore what kind of man your father is?" Dax asked with a shrug.

"Damn it, Dax. Shut up. Maybe it wasn't the best idea to have you here." Ryan cupped Lily's face and made her look at him. "I had no choice but to let him in our wedding. The FBI was very persuasive. In defense of my friend, who I'm not sure deserves it at the moment, he didn't want any part in this. They told me a lot of things your father has done."

"Allegedly," Lily stated with confidence.

"I guess that answers my question. You like to ignore the truth." Two sets of eyes turned daggers at him.

"Lily, sweetheart, listen—"

"Let's break it down for you," Dax interrupted Ryan. He couldn't stand it anymore. Not her naivety, her ignorance, or the bad feeling worming its way to the pit of his stomach. "Your father knows I work for the FBI. He's already put a hit on me. And to sweeten the deal, he's added one for your husband because he brought me in. He's just as guilty in your father's eyes. So you have a choice. Leave with your husband, or take sides with your father?"

A horrifying gasp fell from her lips as her eyes turned to panic. "You're wrong. That's a lie. My father would never do something so horrible."

"Do you honestly believe that, Lily? You've known the man your entire life. Do you really believe he doesn't hurt people?" Dax asked, his voice softening a tiny bit. He didn't mean to be so harsh. Not really. But his fear for Sarafina was suddenly spiking. He'd been gone way too long.

"How do you know all this? Tell me and maybe I'll consider it to be true. Maybe." She moved closer to Ryan, letting him slip an arm around her waist.

He shouldn't. He shouldn't say a damn word. But for her to truly believe him, he had to. "Sarafina. She overheard him on the phone before you got to the house yesterday. That's why she wanted my number. She wanted to warn me."

Lily almost fell to the floor as the horror washed over her face, except Ryan held her tightly to his side, keeping her upright. "Oh my God."

"Do you believe me now?" Dax asked quietly, even though he could see she did.

"I called her this morning. I wanted help with my room. She declined, but I wanted to know if she called you. I know how much she likes you." Lily covered her mouth as a strangled sound escaped. "So I asked. My father was right there. I didn't ask where they were going, but him and Travis left a little before I did."

The air left his body as if he'd just been sucker punched

in the gut. That icky, swarming feeling now made sense. Sarafina needed him.

"Pack your shit. Be ready to leave with those agents outside within ten minutes." He pointed a finger at Lily. "You either choose your husband or you choose your father. You have ten minutes to decide."

He raced for the front door. Ryan's words only stopped him for a second. "Where the hell are you going?"

"To get the woman I love. To make sure he hasn't harmed her. I can't live without her. There's your answer."

---

SARAFINA GLANCED BETWEEN THE TWO, settling her eyes on Travis, who looked hurt, but not frightening like Mr. C.

"You said you had no contact with Dax. Why would you call him?" Travis asked, the pain clear in his voice.

"Perhaps she would like me to answer."

Sarafina slowly looked at Mr. C, his lips curling into a vicious grin. She decided she liked the thin-lip look much better than this one.

"You overheard my conversation, didn't you, my dear Fina?"

"What conversation?" Travis asked, looking between the two.

"I've been trying to teach you the ropes of the business. It hasn't been going as smoothly as I like. Getting arrested already. Very amateur, Travis." Mr. C shook his head. "Daxton Delcroy, Special Agent for the FBI. Isn't that right, Fina?"

"Did you know this?" Travis asked, the pain not only in his voice, but now etched on his face.

"I saw him at the precinct when you were arrested. Yes, I

knew. And yes, I overheard you on the phone, Mr. C. I didn't want to believe you could be a bad man. I didn't." She wiped a tear away. "But when you said you wanted him taken care of and it's unfortunate about Ryan as well, that makes you a bad man. That's your daughter's husband. You're just going to take him away from her?"

"It's business. She'll mourn and she'll move on. She'll have her family by her side." Mr. C shrugged as if it wasn't a big deal he put a hit out for his daughter's husband.

"Shit, Dad. You're not going to kill Ryan, are you? What did he do?"

Mr. C, with a smug-like grin, turned toward Travis. "He brought an FBI agent into our family. At his own damn wedding. If he loved my daughter, your sister, like he said he did, he would've never done that. That's not the Chilani way." He turned toward Sarafina. "I've always thought of you as a daughter. Now is your chance to prove that you're part of the family. Did you call Dax? And if so, what did you say to him?"

Another tear slid down. How could she possibly answer that? This man, a man she had known since she was a little girl, was about to kill her. A cruel, heartless man. How had she been so blind?

"Your silence is answer enough, Fina. I'm truly disappointed in you. This almost breaks my heart." Mr. C pulled a gun from his jacket.

"Shit, you're not really going to kill Fina, are you?" Travis asked as he took a step closer to her.

Mr. C shook his head. "Of course not." He walked farther into the living room and shoved the weapon into his hands. "You are."

Sarafina stumbled back, almost tripping over the coffee

table. Travis glanced at her, then back at his father. "This is ridiculous, Dad. I can't—"

"You will or you're dead to me. You've been resisting taking over this entire operation and I'm done. You show me that you have what it takes to run this business. You show me right now. She betrayed the family. One of the most important jobs in this family is to keep it together. She slept with him. It's written all over her face. How does that make you feel, Travis?" Mr. C stepped back, raising his brows with curiosity.

She couldn't stop the downfall of tears. They were silent, but they were there. Travis couldn't possibly do this. She couldn't believe Mr. C wanted him to do it.

"Please, Travis..." Pleading might not work, but she had to try.

He stared at the gun, then looked at her. "Did you sleep with him?"

She was going to die. She could see it in his eyes. The pain. Why didn't she see this sooner? No sense in lying anymore. "Yes."

"Do you know how long I've loved you? And not as a brother." The gun shook in his hand as his voice wavered a bit.

"I have no idea."

He raised the gun, pointing it straight at her chest. "For the longest time. I was too scared to admit the truth. I love you, Sarafina."

"I love you, Travis. I'm sorry it's not in the way you want."

"Me, too."

The loud sound of the gunshot rang throughout the house.

## 15

DAX'S HEART stopped beating the exact moment the gunshot echoed around him. Ears ringing, hands shaking, mind disoriented, he whipped his gun out from behind his jacket and threw open the front door.

It took only two steps to see his world shift, yet again.

"Put the gun down, Travis."

A pair of eyes, muddy brown, filled with pain and heartache, looked at him. "Special Agent Daxton Delcroy. This is your fault."

Dax took another step. "Do you really believe that? Please put the gun down. I don't want to shoot you. For Sarafina's sake." He glanced at her, offering a smile that everything would be okay.

And it would be. Everything would be okay. She unharmed. Safe. Protected. Damn if he didn't love her like there was no tomorrow.

"I killed my father," Travis said in a trance, his eyes glued to Martin Chilani lying in the middle of the living room with a bullet hole dead center in his chest.

"And you saved Sarafina's life, didn't you?"

Travis's eyes jerked toward him as the gun leveled at his chest. "I hate you. I won't let anyone hurt her. Nobody. That includes you."

"I would never hurt her," Dax said calmly, then chanced a glance her way. She stood with silent tears streaming down her face, her eyes glazed with terror. Like Travis had been doing when he busted in, she also couldn't tear her eyes away from Martin Chilani. Not even the brief smile he gave her had dissuaded her from staring at his body.

"Are you sure about that? Did you call her the next morning? Or was she just a pawn to take down my family?" Travis took a step toward him, the gun steady in his hand.

Dax raised his hands, gun high in the air. "Shoot me, Travis. If it'll make you feel better. I deserve it. I didn't call her."

"Travis, no," Sarafina cried, rushing toward him.

Dax kept his hands in the air, even as the painful urge to pull her away from Travis came over him. He deserved a bullet to the chest. He hurt her. Every time he left before morning, or left in general, he hurt her. Look at what leaving her this morning created. It put her in the path of danger. As much as he wanted to lower his weapon and aim it straight at Travis's heart, he held his hands in the air while her hand clung to Travis's arm, yet she didn't reach for the gun. Travis didn't look at her, his eyes glued to him.

"He hurt you, didn't he?" Travis finally looked at her. "I can't believe my father would ask me to kill you. I could never hurt you. I'll never let anyone else hurt you either."

"He didn't. I swear. Please put the gun down."

"He didn't call." Travis's brow rose. He didn't ask a question, but he still acted like he needed an answer.

"He showed up. That's more important than a phone call." Sarafina looked at Dax, finally offering a tentative smile, then looked back at Travis. "I'm sorry about your father. I would've never asked you to make that kind of decision."

Travis's hand wavered. "I know you wouldn't. You thought I was going to shoot you, didn't you?"

Her hand slid down his arm, grasping the gun. "I was prepared for it, but I know you're not your father. Any bad thing he did doesn't reflect on you. You're a good man."

Travis let the gun go as Sarafina gripped it firmly. "You are truly the perfect woman. I wish you loved me instead of him."

"I'm sorry." The tears had abated, but a lone tear slid down her cheek.

Travis wiped it away. "Don't be. I'll kill him if he ever hurts you." He glanced at Dax, his eyes reinforcing his words.

Dax nodded as he slowly lowered his hands. He'd take the threat. If the time ever came that he hurt her, he'd want nothing more than Travis to end his pain. That was the last thing he'd ever do.

"I need a drink. I sure hope you still have the bottle of scotch I left here, Fina." Travis walked past Dax without flinching or fear that he would slap handcuffs on him for shooting his father.

That was the last thing on his mind. Although, it should be front and center. The only thing he wanted was standing a few feet from him. He rushed to Sarafina and took the gun from her wobbly hands, setting it down on the coffee table. Wrapping her tightly in his arms, he let the tremors settle, soothing her as best as he could.

"You can't arrest him, Dax. Please…he didn't mean—"

Dax kissed her. Lightly. Tenderly. Enough to quiet her words that came out in trembles. "I know self-defense when

I see it. You always, since the beginning, told me he would never hurt you. I don't doubt that anymore. He'll never see a jail cell if I have anything to do with it." He kissed her again, to give himself more reassurance that she was okay. "Because he chose to save you over his father. And for that, he'll never see me gunning for him again."

"Thank you."

"Are you okay? I'm sorry I ever left."

Her eyes glided to the body on the floor. "I…"

He grabbed her hand and walked her out of the living room and into the hallway that led to the kitchen. "I really need to call this in, but I need to know you're okay first."

"I don't know how I feel. Mr. C's telling Travis he better shoot or he's dead to him. He had the gun pointed at me. I thought he was going to shoot."

He rubbed his hands up and down her arms, the tremors still sparking off like fireworks. "You're an amazing woman. That's why he didn't. I'm sorry. For everything."

"It's not your fault."

A lame laugh burst out, echoing around the tiny hallway. "A little bit. Your life was normal, carefree before I came." Rubbing his jaw, he shook his head. "I wish I could erase these last few minutes for you. You should've never had to endure that."

"And you shouldn't have to run anymore."

He shrugged. "That remains to be seen, but you're probably right. Technically, with Martin out of the picture, Travis is head of the business now."

"He'll fix it. He'll take care of it."

"Are you sure you don't love him? At the wedding…"

She stroked a hand across his cheek. "I'll always love him. But he doesn't have my heart like you do."

"That's something that makes me very happy to hear. Ryan asked if I could live without you. I was prepared to run without you by my side. I thought that would be the best way to protect you." He pulled her tightly into his embrace. "I'm an idiot sometimes. I hope you can forgive me when I act that way."

Her lips tipped up into a beautiful grin. "What are you saying, Dax?"

"That I can't live without you. That I love you with all my heart. I need you to keep me safe. Only you can do that properly. That walk down the aisle nearly killed me, but not with you hanging tightly to my arm."

"I love you, too. But I thought it was your job to keep me safe?"

He kissed her lightly, slipping his tongue in for a brief taste. "I kind of like how we keep each other safe. You do the aisle thing better than me. Walk down the aisle with me again. I need the practice."

She leaned back, brows dipping, as if she were trying to decipher his words. "Are you…"

"Yeah, I am." Smiling wide, he pulled her in for another kiss. "Marry me, Sarafina."

"Damn, already?"

He turned his head to Travis, who stood in the hallway with a glass in his hand. The torment written on his face couldn't be faked or erased. At the moment, Dax didn't care. "Would you honestly give her a chance to get away?"

Travis chugged his glass back, his face grim. "Hell, no." He tossed his head toward the living room. "About my father…I didn't want to do what I did. But there's no way he would've let either of us walk out of the house if I didn't. I don't know everything, but what I do know, the information is all yours."

Dax nodded. "I guess I should call this in. I got distracted."

Travis swirled the ice in his glass, then slowly lifted his lips into a grin. "Yeah, Fina has that affect on people. Don't forget what I said."

"Loud and clear. I'll hand you the gun myself." And he would. He'd rather die than hurt Sarafina in any way. A quick nod from Travis and he knew he read his mind.

---

A WARM HAND curled around hers that were clasped in her lap. Lifting her head, she burst into tears at the sorrowful face staring back. "Lily, I'm so sorry."

Lily sat down and hugged her. "Fina, none of this is your fault. Are you okay?"

She pulled away, wiping the tears with a quick swipe of her hand. Pathetic. Here, Lily's father was dead, and she was making it about her. She should be wiping Lily's tears away. Why wasn't she crying?

"I wish people would stop asking me that. I'm fine. I should be asking you that question. Your father—"

"Became not worthy of my affections when he told his people to kill Ryan. When he told my brother to kill you. Screw him. Are you okay? Because I'm still shaking a little here. I think I need another vacation with Ryan to sort out my feelings."

"Do it. Get away for a while. I'm still in shock myself. Poor Travis has been in that interrogation room for so long."

Lily looked down the hallway. Sarafina's gaze followed. She lost track of the time. She had absolutely no idea how long she'd been at the FBI headquarters. She refused to be swayed when Dax told her she didn't need to come with.

One look and he knew he wouldn't win that argument. Travis needed her. Dax needed her. And the most important part, she needed them more than anything else.

"Perhaps you need to get away." Lily squeezed her hand. "With someone special. Someone I actually wanted to bash over the head with a frying pan until he dashed out of the house like his world was ending."

Sarafina turned to her, brows dipping into confusion. "A frying pan? What did he do?"

"He's not the brightest when delivering news."

"He doesn't like to talk. His last relationship didn't last because he never talked."

Lily side bumped her. "Bet you get him to talk with ease."

She laughed and bit her bottom lip to stop the smile from becoming bigger. "He might've said he couldn't live without me. That he loves me. Maybe even said marry me."

Lily slapped a hand over her mouth to squash the squeal that wanted to escape. "What did you say?"

"It wasn't good timing. I haven't answered."

"Well, what are you going to say?"

"We barely know each other. And I think I should reserve that answer for him."

Lily leaned against the wall. "Maybe it hasn't been long, but you remember when I met Ryan, don't you? That festival in Central Park. Two weeks and I knew he was the one for me. The only reason I didn't follow my heart was because I knew how my dad would react."

"Yeah, but he didn't ask you to marry him right away, did he?"

"No. But I would've asked him. I knew. I can't explain it. Follow your heart, Fina. He's an idiot with words, but he loves you. That was pretty clear."

An hour later, Sarafina was wandering the hallways trying to pass the time and not lose her mind. After visiting with Lily and Ryan, and still no news on how long Travis would be, she needed a small breather to herself.

Travis had said he would tell Dax everything he knew. She was proud of him for that. Never once did she doubt he was a good man. Well, okay. She might have doubted it for a brief moment when he pointed the gun at her. Then, like a flash of lightning, he swiveled the gun toward his father and boom. The loudest noise imaginable echoed around her. The way crimson blossomed out a teeny tiny hole and slowly trickled down like a lazy river. Mr. C had stood frozen for what seemed like minutes before collapsing to the ground.

She hadn't known what to do after that. Did she check for a pulse? Did she hug Travis and thank him? Did she comfort him? Nothing but terror had entered her mind. Then, nothing mattered. Dax burst into the house, and all she wanted to do was run into his arms.

"We gotta stop doing this. It's becoming a habit. Although, it's not a bad one when I really think about it. It puts you in my arms," Dax whispered as he pulled her farther into his arms after she bumped into him.

Clearly, she hadn't been paying attention to her surroundings. Daydreaming. More like reliving a nightmare. Thankfully, she ran into Dax when her mind drifted away from her.

A light kiss and a tender caress down her back soothed her nerves that she hadn't realized were so coiled together she probably could've burst at any moment.

"You shouldn't be here. We have your statement. You look tired." Dax grabbed her cheeks, rubbing his thumbs, as his face flashed a myriad of emotions. "Talk to me, Sarafina."

"You hate talking."

"It's not so bad when I'm talking to you."

"I am tired. But I want…"

Dropping her eyes, she couldn't seem to find it in her to finish that sentence. Fear. Again. So much fear.

"You want to wait for Travis. He's almost done. Just writing a few more things down. He refused to talk to anyone but me. That's why I haven't been checking on you like I wanted to. I wasn't trying to avoid you or anything."

"He gets to go home?"

Dax dropped his hands and shoved one through his hair. "Yeah. All charges for his arrest a few weeks ago have been dropped. He's a free man. The information he provided should help us take down a lot of people. It'll be a long process, though. My favorite part is, I don't have to leave. Travis is the boss now. He assured me he'd put a stop to the hits out against me and Ryan. I believe him. Plus, once we get most of Martin Chilani's men off the streets, it shouldn't be an issue."

He started to run another hand through his hair when she grabbed it. "So no running. What do you—" Wow, this was hard. She blew a breath. "I want you to take me home. I want you to stay."

"Here I thought I was still competing with Travis."

"You've never competed with him. You've always been the only one. Did you mean what you said earlier?"

A sweet grin grew as he pulled her in for a kiss. A slow, delicious kiss that told her without words that he meant what he said. Her body shifted closer and molded perfectly to his frame. Every hard inch touched her, bringing the burning desire front and center. Now she really wanted him to take her home.

"I want to find a closet. Have my wicked way with you," he whispered, then peppered a few sensual kisses down her neck and back to her mouth.

"Maybe we do need to work on this talking business you don't like to do."

He laughed with her. "I meant what I said. Problem is, you haven't answered my question."

She shrugged, yet her smile never wavered. "It sounded more like a statement at the time."

"Is this payback for all the times I left before morning? Holding me in my misery? Extending the suspense?"

"No. You were never anything but honest. I should've never expected more. That's on me."

He sighed. "Sarafina, I'm—"

"Yes, I'll marry you."

A smile so wide grew on his face that she couldn't help but kiss him. Tossing her arms around him, she jumped and wrapped her legs as tightly as she could. "I'm ready for that closet now."

"One closet coming right up," he whispered against her lips as they laughed together.

Two feet ahead of him, he found the perfect closet.

## 16

DAX TRIED to draw in a decent breath as his friend and partner fiddled with his bow tie. "Could you hurry up? You're choking me here."

"Damn thing won't stay straight. I'm no bow expert."

Swiping his hand, he finally inhaled a deep breath. Colt laughed as he took a step back. "I don't think it's customary to kill the groom right before he's about to get married."

"Tell me. Is it customary to kill one of the guests before the ceremony?" Colt asked as his face became rigid, his lips pressed together so tightly that Dax wasn't sure how one word slipped out.

He followed Colt's gaze to where Travis laughed with his sister. His hand touched her shoulder and she appeared to lean farther into him until Dax almost thought she would tip over soon.

"He's not so bad. He might even make a decent brother-in-law."

Colt slowly turned his head. "If you weren't one of my best friends, I'd coldcock you right now. You do realize he's the head of the Chilani family now. Hell, look at your side of the aisle. Basically, all law enforcement. Now look at her side of the aisle. Half are associated with the mob. And you say he's not so bad."

Dax glanced to where Lily stood with Ryan and her sister Lora. That was the extent of the Chilani family in attendance. He wouldn't necessarily say half of her side was associated with the mob. Lora didn't hold a grudge against Travis or Sarafina for what happened to her father. Although, Lora was single-minded and selfish. Dax figured she was glad her father was out of the picture so she could do anything she damn well pleased without anyone to stop her. Not even her mother could stop her anymore.

Mrs. Chilani hadn't taken it so well. Since the incident, she had disowned Travis and rarely spoke to Lily and Lora. She had basically locked herself inside her home, conversing with very few people. The people she did associate with concerned Dax. One of them being Franklin, who, thus far, had managed to avoid arrest. They hadn't managed to arrest all of Martin Chilani's men yet. Building evidence took time.

Travis was the head of the operation now. As far as Dax knew, he was slowly trying to make his father's business legit. With the help of the FBI, he had been doing a decent job. Of course, with any operation, there were always a few problems.

Mrs. Chilani was one of them.

Dax didn't want to worry about any of that right now. Not today.

"Travis isn't bad. You know that. He's been helping us bring down the Chilani operation. So, worry number one checked off. Considering there are only about ten to fifteen people on each side of the aisle, I wouldn't say half are associated with the mob. And third, Travis saved her life. He'll always be good in my eyes. Now fix the damn bow tie without choking me."

Colt laughed as he stepped closer and attempted one more time to make the bow tie as straight as possible. "As my friend, you could at least tell Travis that my sister is off-limits."

"Oh, you're not afraid of him, are you? Tell him your-self." Dax coughed once, then glared as best as he could standing so close to Colt. "Note to self. Don't say shit like that when you have your hands around my neck."

"Good idea, buddy."

"What's a good idea?" Ryan asked as he slapped a hand on Dax's shoulder.

Dax shoved Colt's hands away again. "You fixing my bow tie is a good idea. This idiot has no idea what he's doing."

Ryan laughed, then went to tackle the bow tie. "I see Travis is taking a liking to your sister, Colt."

"I'm trying to pretend that's not happening. Can we change the subject? Like, shit. How in the hell did you do that so fast?" Colt said as Ryan stepped away from Dax, the bow neatly tied and precision straight.

"I've been married before. Plus, I've been to way too many functions requiring a bow tie. Nothing to it."

"Thank you, Ryan. I'm ready. Where's my bride?" Dax said, his eyes searching the room like he was on a stakeout and needed to pay attention to everything going on around him.

"Regretting the fact she's marrying you. Vegas? Really?"

Dax turned around and smiled at Travis. "You don't like the little chapel we picked?"

"It's Vegas. Fina doesn't strike me as the type to get married in Vegas. She deserves better." Travis held his ground. Dax had to give him props for that, especially with Ryan and Colt standing there as well.

"Deserves better than me, you mean?"

Travis shared a look with Ryan, then turned back to him. "Not really. You make her happy, so that's all that matters to me. She deserves a big wedding full of beautiful things. Not tacky ridiculousness. At least this minister, or whoever the hell that guy is up there, isn't dressed like Elvis."

Dax chuckled. "She actually wanted Elvis, but I talked her out of it."

"Yeah, right." Travis crossed his arms.

"Trust me, Travis. Do you think I give a shit where I get married, as long as I get to marry her?"

Travis whipped his arms wide. "Fina honestly wanted to get married in this little rinky-dink chapel in Las Vegas? No bridesmaids. No groomsmen. Just a small guest list."

"She did. And what Sarafina wants, Sarafina gets." Dax slapped him on the shoulder. "This is what she wanted. Hey, you know what Colt wants?"

Colt groaned and backed up while Travis furrowed his brows, then shifted his gaze to a petite blonde in a pink dress. "She's smart, beautiful, and very nice."

Colt took a step closer to him, pointing his finger. "Exactly. My sister is nice. Unwritten rule, you don't take nice girls home from a wedding."

Travis grinned like the devil. "Good thing we're in Vegas. Not possible to take her home." He shrugged, yet his smile never wavered. "I know the rule. Fina would kick my ass."

"I would, too. Although, perhaps I should know what we're talking about so I know why I'm kicking your ass," Dominic said, joining the small circle.

Dax grinned at Dominic and the way he was protective of Sarafina. She had so many men who cared about her. He couldn't believe how lucky he was that she picked *him* to love with all her heart.

"The rule. You wouldn't know about it, since, you know..." Travis shrugged, yet smirked.

Dominic's brow rose. "Since I'm what? Gay?"

"Yeah. Since you're that."

Dax normally found it very amusing these two never got along. Not even after Travis saved Sarafina's life did Dominic take a liking to Travis. But today it wasn't acceptable. Nothing would ruin her day. He cleared his throat. "Gentlemen, let's keep it peaceful. For Sarafina."

"Of course, Dax. I saw your friend struggling with your bow tie, but I see it's been fixed." Dominic smiled politely.

"Ryan to the rescue," Dax replied.

"Good. I just finished checking on Sarafina. She's almost ready. Are you?" Dominic asked.

"I've been ready since I asked her." He would've married her the same day if he could've.

"You make her happy. I'm so glad she met you." Dominic winked and then turned to Travis with his hand outstretched. "Truce for the weekend."

Travis eyed his hand warily, then shook it. "Truce."

"I'm going to grab my seat by Freddie. Perhaps you all should as well." Dominic walked away.

"Who made him the boss?" Travis watched Dominic take a seat, his tone of voice insinuating he considered himself the only boss around.

"Truce, remember, Travis?" Dax said, wondering if maybe being in charge of his father's business was starting to get to his head. They still had a ways to go to completely diminish the business. He needed Travis to stay on the straight and narrow. Of course, if he voiced any of that concern to Sarafina, she'd say he had nothing to worry about when it came to Travis.

So he wouldn't worry.

"You know I can't stand—never mind. I'm going to take my seat by the beautiful woman I was talking to earlier. Maybe I am ready for a nice girl." He smiled at Colt and walked away.

Colt continued to glare daggers at Travis's back. "Why do I feel like he's going to flirt with my sister all evening?"

Dax nudged Colt toward the chairs. "You're all here for three more days. Might not just be for the evening."

Colt shook his fist as Ryan laughed. Dax started to walk backwards. "Take your seats, gentlemen. I'm about to get married."

Ryan slapped him on the back for luck and then joined Lily, who had already taken a seat.

Colt grinned deviously at him as he started to walk away. "You're a dead man when you come home from your honeymoon. Beware. You have no idea what I'll do to you when you step into the office."

Dax shrugged and grinned wickedly, then turned around. He wasn't too worried. No matter how many pranks they played on each other at work, their friendship never wavered. He couldn't wait to see what crazy thing Colt came up with. The look on his face had been worth it.

And really, Travis wasn't that bad of a guy. After taking three months to get to know him, he was starting to get used to him. At first, it annoyed him that Travis wanted to be around Sarafina so much. It didn't take long to realize that Travis was a friend to her and she wanted only him. Nobody but him.

At times, it amazed him that he got so lucky. Maybe it hadn't been long since they met, but he knew getting married so soon was the right decision. He couldn't let her get away. She was the best thing he ever ran into.

"So is this how we're starting the ceremony?" a sweet voice whispered.

He looked into the eyes of the most beautiful woman who was about to become his wife. "It wouldn't be right to start the day without running into you at least once. That's how we met." He kissed her sweetly on the lips. "Travis didn't believe me that you wanted to get married here. You do, right?"

She nodded. "And I want to walk down the aisle with you. That was one of my favorite parts at Lily's wedding. I was definitely safe in your arms. I almost fell flat on my face. I don't want a fairytale ending like everyone else. I want my own kind of fairytale."

"Not gonna happen on my watch."

He argued with her at first about walking her down the aisle. It should be her father who had that honor. But Sarafina assured him she knew what she wanted and that her father didn't mind. She wanted *him* to walk her down the aisle. So he quit arguing. What Sarafina wanted for her special day, she got.

He took a step back and took in her entire dress.

Gorgeous. A pure hidden gem that he couldn't believe he found.

The top of her dress, heart shaped and strapless, was white with glittering beads that brightened the room. The bottom half was sewn together with many different colors. Thirteen to be exact. The precise number of times she was a bridesmaid. Her mother had taken all of her bridesmaid's dresses and made the bottom portion of her dress with them. Layered in blues, greens, yellows, reds, pinks, gold, and one color that she told him was chartreuse. He had never heard of it. A weird looking yellow-greenish color, that no matter how strange it looked or sounded to pronounce, looked absolutely stunning on her.

So beautiful. So colorful. So original. Exactly the way she wanted it. She didn't want the typical wedding with a white dress and bridal party. It was her turn to get married and she informed him right away she wanted everything different. She wanted it to be something she would remember forever. He had nodded and then kissed her senseless. He didn't care about the details, as long as she became his wife.

Talking was overrated anyway. She was still working with him on that. But unlike Bridget, she was okay when he didn't talk. Kisses were a much better form of communication.

"I have no words. This...you're exquisite." He grabbed her hands and twirled her once. The dress swirled like a beautiful rainbow in a kaleidoscope, the colors blending and bouncing off each other.

"I don't look silly?" Sarafina ran a hand down the dress as she laughed nervously.

"Never."

She cupped his face and planted a scorching kiss on his lips. "And you think you don't have a way with words. I love you."

Oh, how he wished the honeymoon was about to start. He grasped her waist and pulled her closer. "I love you. How about we walk down the aisle and then run to our hotel room? I'm dying to see what's underneath this dress. Perhaps like the last wedding we attended. A white lacy thong?"

She extracted herself from his embrace and looped an arm through his. "Let's take that walk."

They started walking toward the red carpet that announced the start of the blissful walk he'd been waiting to take for the last three months. He nodded at a woman with a crazy looking fedora hat with a feather sticking out of the side sitting on the piano bench and waited for the music to start.

Everyone turned to look at them and stood up. His friends, who were more like family than anything else. Her family and friends. The people who mattered the most. That's all they wanted for their special day.

The music slowly drifted toward them.

"You're sure your father was okay letting me walk down the aisle with you?" Dax whispered before he took one step.

"Yep. This is what I want. Just you and me. Bride and groom."

He kissed her neck, his lips lingering and aching to trail downward. "You never did answer my question."

She took the first step toward the altar, requiring him to follow her movement. "I didn't think it'd be wise to tell you I have nothing on underneath the dress. We might've never made the walk down the aisle, then."

Stumbling in his steps, she kept him from falling flat on his face. "Sarafina..."

"I saved you this time."

He stopped at the altar, held a finger up to the man standing in front of them in a white jacket and pants, and pulled her closer. "You can save me anytime. But you're so in for it when we're done here. I love you so damn much."

"No bra either. Did I mention that?" she winked and turned toward the man. "We're ready."

He pulled her into his side and squeezed. Definitely not ready. He wanted to find the nearest closet and have his wicked way with her. Instead, he focused on the words before him and followed the motions. The sooner they finished this, the sooner he could get her deliriously naked.

And just like that, she went from a beautiful bride to his enchanting wife.

---

LOOKING FOR ANOTHER GREAT ROMANTIC SUSPENSE? START MY LUCKY TOWN SERIES WITH ESCAPING MEMORIES!

For an exciting Romantic Suspense
Escaping Memories
A Lucky Town Novel, #1

*Her past is a deadly puzzle she must solve...before it's too late.*

Stumbling into a stranger's isolated cabin, she's terrified—
her memories a dangerous blank slate. The only thing her
instincts scream is to trust the ruggedly handsome Sheriff
Logan Caldwell who found her. With his protective nature
and gentle touch, he also makes her feel safer than she has
in...well, as long as she can remember.

As shadows of her forgotten past close in, Logan becomes
her only ally against an unknown enemy. Every recovered
memory brings more fear than answers. As passion ignites
between them, one thing becomes clear: if her enemy finds
her, she'll meet a fate worse than death.

*With nail-biting suspense and smoldering romance, plunge into
the danger and desire with the first book in the Lucky Town series
today!*

For An Exciting Contemporary Romance
## THE WRONG BROTHER
A PERFECT FOR YOU NOVEL, #1

**Objective:** Get hired as a temporary secretary and find out if Champ Holloway is a dirty, cheating scumbag.
**Time Frame:** One week.

Gabby would do anything for her best friend, Mia. Anything. That's what besties are for, right? But going undercover at her boyfriend's work to find out if he's cheating seems a bit extreme. Except she can't say no. Never to Mia. The moment she walks in and sees her *boyfriend*, she knows she made a mistake. He's sex on a stick, and she wants to take a delicious bite. He's also a bit too arrogant, needs to work on his pleases and thank yous, and he never smiles. Everyone should smile at least once a day. It's one long week of a battle of wills, sinful glances, and keeping her hands to herself. All she can do is repeat Mia. Mia. Mia. This is all for Mia. Until she realizes...there are two Mr. Holloways. And she got hired by the wrong one.

*Warning: This is not a full romcom. While it has moments of humor, it also has a twist of angst. Okay, now you can dive in, you're prepared!*

# ABOUT THE AUTHOR

I'm a *USA Today* Bestselling Author that loves to write contemporary romance and romantic suspense novels, although I am partial to romantic suspense. I even dabble in paranormal. Honestly, I love anything that has to do with romance. As long as there's a happy ending, I'm a happy camper. And insta-love...yes, please! I love baseball (Go Twins!) and creating awesome crafts. I graduated with a Bachelor's Degree in Criminal Justice, working in that field for several years before I became a stay-at-home mom. I have a few more amazing stories in the works. If you would like to learn more about me and my books, head to my website by scanning the QR code. Thanks for reading!

*Scan me*

www.ingramcontent.com/pod-product-compliance
Lightning Source LLC
Chambersburg PA
CBHW030333030726
47499CB00003B/755